Ink

Ink

A Novel

Angela Woodward

UNIVERSITY PRESS OF KENTUCKY

Scholarly publisher for the Commonwealth, serving Bellarmine University,
Berea College, Centre College of Kentucky, Eastern Kentucky University,
The Filson Historical Society, Georgetown College, Kentucky Historical Society,
Kentucky State University, Morehead State University, Murray State University,
Northern Kentucky University, Spalding University, Transylvania University,
University of Kentucky, University of Louisville, University of Pikeville,
and Western Kentucky University.

Editorial and Sales Offices: The University Press of Kentucky
663 South Limestone Street, Lexington, Kentucky 40508-4008
www.kentuckypress.com

Names: Woodward, Angela, 1962– author.
Title: Ink : a novel / Angela Woodward.
Description: Lexington : University Press of Kentucky, [2023] | Series: University
    press of Kentucky new poetry & prose series
Identifiers: LCCN 2022034833 | ISBN 9780813196534 (hardcover ; acid-free paper) |
    ISBN 9780813196541 (pdf) | ISBN 9780813196558 (epub)
Subjects: LCGFT: Novels.
Classification: LCC PS3623.O6825 I55 2023 | DDC 813/.6—dc23/eng/20220725
LC record available at https://lccn.loc.gov/2022034833

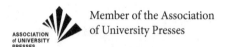

Member of the Association
of University Presses

For Isabel and Abner

Ink

Ink obscures its nature. Let's focus on the substance itself, rather than the marks it makes. Ink can be blue or black, or any color, even white. It can be eked out of a pen nib, or sprayed onto a moving page by tiny, precise nozzles. People or their machines have compacted it into plastic cartridges, or stuffed it down into a bottle, or scraped it from a solid wedge onto a stone and then moistened it. The first act of calligraphy is the writer's rhythmic rubbing of the dry ink across a rough surface. The writer begins by calming the hand, preparing it for its exertions.

A story could begin, "They took me into a room and beat me." The story could go on, "On another occasion I was forced to lie down while MPs jumped onto my back and legs." It might continue, "In the foregoing parts of this memorandum we have demonstrated . . ." and from there, we could stop.

The inexpert writer may have mixed her ink too thin, and her composition will show weak streaks and drips. If she has not thoroughly and patiently prepared, uneven glops will show up in her writing like underlinings or exclamation points, clumsy emphasis. Typewriter ribbons, soaked in ink and then dried like noodles, rotate around their spools. They give of their essence, transferring dark blots onto the page behind them. It can go on this way for months, until they are used up by the repeated strikes of tiny metal mallets.

The Material

A story could begin, "They took me into a room and beat me." The story could go on, "They started to hit me on my broken leg several times with a solid plastic stick."

The writer has been working with this material for quite some time. What astonishes her is the way it lies around, available to any of us. Despite the protracted fight to keep these documents and photos out of the public record, some small percentage of them made their way into newspapers and onto websites years ago. The idea of a nation's dark secrets lying buried beneath the floorboards has been totally transformed into a new metaphor of an unlocked warehouse. Anyone can walk around in it, dazed by the glare of the sulfurous floodlights. A baton here, a pool of urine there, a transcript of a medical exam, pictures and captions. The writer has to make an effort to close her eyes, or to squint briefly at some intervening object, or to find a negative pattern in the interstices between these appalling records, as there's no art to simply revealing what's already there.

Or so I said to myself maybe five or six years ago.

Ink

The ink maker begins in the woods, cutting hawthorn. The hawthorn branches are next peeled and the bark soaked in water. This water is boiled down until it blackens, then is mixed with wine. The maker of ink may be making wine simultaneously, in another vessel. Alternatively, ink can be made from the galls that swell on oaks when certain wasps lay eggs in them. The wasp's hormones provoke the oak into blistering, and this round protrusion protects the wasp family as the larvae grow. Their home shelters and feeds them, until at last the larvae change form. They were worms, bound to one spot, and now they fly around in the open, graceful bodies ending with a pen-like point.

Or this—men and women study extensively in universities and then are hired by tech companies. There they conspire to illuminate different-colored capsules, some black, some white, in an imitation of paper and the words written on it. The human eye can't see these individual capsules without magnification. They hover beneath the surface of the glass book, turning and rising, then dropping away in a complex pattern choreographed by the alphabet. Words, sentences, whole book-length memoranda command these capsules to bob and sink. Maybe one minuscule white one was for a brief moment next to a black one within the letter *r* within the word *room* within a translated and transcribed interview session that begins, "They took me into a room and beat me. They tied me to the window with my hands behind my back until I lost consciousness." The person reading touches the bottom of the screen and the microcapsules fall, turn, twist, and rise into a completely new configuration so quickly the reader doesn't even notice. This action seems to go on ceaselessly, with ease, like breathing.

In yet another method of making ink, maids collected the soot from lamps and sold it down the alley to the soot dealer. The soot clung to their fingers and entered their mouths as they ate. They wiped their runny noses with the backs of their hands. In fact the maids' faces, and the faces of their siblings and children, were coated with a thin film of black at all times, cleared only by tears. In this way, moments of sorrow wrote themselves on their cheeks, briefly.

For most of history, the users of ink would have been only a few accountants. Schoolchildren wrote with chalk on slate. What they inscribed one hour was gone the next. The school principal threatened little Jack with a mark on his permanent record, because only he had the means to write *Poor Behavior* in letters that might fade to brown but still be legible thirty years later.

The writings of the poor have been mostly impeded by lack of time, but also by lack of heat. In winter, the ink freezes in the bottle. The writer begins by holding the ink container in her armpit. Sometimes the most magical thoughts cease to appear because of ice crystals. A word is followed not by the next right and appropriate, perhaps brilliant, word, but by a gap and a shard of ice. Two things couldn't be more different, ice and ink. One melts without a trace, one is created only to make traces.

Ice

Among my many books on polar expeditions, I found a description of a ship lost near Greenland around 1855. On a bright, clear day, the captain had his breakfast served on deck so he could observe his ship passing through a last thin lead in the ice before entering a wide, safe, open waterway beyond. While he ate, two floes on either side came together and caught the *Princess Charlotte*. Within ten minutes, the whole ship had sunk beneath the ice. "Everything looks so bright, so calm, so still," the captain wrote, "that it requires positive experience to convince one that ice only a very few inches, perhaps only three or four inches *above water*, perfectly level and moving extremely slow, could possibly endanger a strong vessel."

We find pollen suspended in ice, and dust, traces of pesticides, spores and seeds, radiation. All this is kept still and safe, or so we think, but it melts, flows in glacial sheets downhill, circulates with the ocean currents. Ice buckles up and heaves due to geothermal activity far below. Wind sculpts it into ridges and hollows it into tables. It grows coarse beards. It drips off house eaves. It's a particularly dangerous impermanence—to fall through the ice into Lake Monona, the lake behind my house, would mean death within minutes. The muscles of the fingers freeze so quickly that the hand can't grasp a rope thrown in rescue.

A century ago, blanketed horses pulled ice cutters on Monona, carving the frozen lake into blocks. Men tossed the ice onto railcars and sent them south and east for breweries and meatpackers to cool their goods. Through this rough industrial process, Wisconsin's winter shed its glow on dark shelves in Memphis warehouses. Little boys interrupted their skating to watch the men at work. They longed to grow up to have those muscled shoulders, to wear a long, ragged coat with knobby wrists sticking out of their sleeves. Their little sisters were not allowed near. They were at home, sewing in dim light.

This same water in summer is coated with so much green goo that special paddleboats come out and chop the mats of algae to clear it. Barely a swan could swim, otherwise. All of that is obliterated in January. What a peaceful time, all that life locked down into one flat expanse. I've at times walked almost all the way across Lake Monona, raising a glove now and then to another trudging figure in the distance. I've followed bike tire tracks, and the twin blades of iceboats. Far off, always farther than I can go, a few little shacks send smoke up their chimneys: ice fishermen, sitting on camp stools, waiting.

When there's not too much snow on top, I've looked through the ice at the sandy lake bed and ribbons of seaweed and seen perch move slowly along the bottom. Once I took both kids across the ice to see a kite festival set up in the middle of the lake. The kids got tired, and we turned back long before we got to the swept and fenced-off area where the kite flyers stood ringed by their gear. We saw a few kites—a boat, a rainbow—swooping in the distance, not enough to draw us on. All our boots leaked, and the kids cried and whined about how cold they were. I should have driven them, on the streets, along the shore, and not set straight across. I was sorry we'd even tried it. They were too little then.

In another book in my polar exploration library, a captain recalled finding the topmast of a wooden ship poking out of the ice. A thin, crystalline rime clung to the wood. The mast's straight line, and the ninety-degree angle of the spars, set a forlorn geometry against the tangled undulations of the ice. Beneath the mast, the captain saw the hollow impression a ship had made, stamped into the side of the floating berg. This ship-shaped cavity traveled along, precise in every detail of plank and bolt, its carriage through the water almost as upright as the vessel that had molded it.

Typists

A woman crouched on the floor with an X-Acto knife and ripped through layers of clear packing tape. She set the blade down on the corner of the desk, where it stayed buried under folders and papers for the next several months. She reached into the box and drew out a cassette. The smell from the cardboard reminded her of something to do with schools and lockers. She had thought there might be a scent of origin about the box, something foreign, a bit of sand, petals of desert bloom. Instead, this odor came from bureaucracy, the sanitizing sawdust of orderliness.

"Sylvia," her coworker called. They each had their own box.

The two of them conferred over changing the typewriter ribbon. They had trained on machines like this when they were younger, but had spent their more recent careers laboring on modern instruments with glass screens, autocorrect, and the capacity to wipe out words and whole lines with no repercussions at all. For this contract, they needed to insert carbonless triplicate forms between the rollers of the IBM Selectric. It was a pain compared to working on a computer, but parts of the bureaucracy still relied on routing these pages by hand to different offices. The decision to use typewriters had likely been made by someone older, higher up, who failed to see any flaw in a system that had worked perfectly for years. It had hardly been a decision, but just the accepted means to an end. Or it had been the deferral of a decision to make a change, from typing on the forms to creating a template using a word-processing program and emailing a document to each interested party. Someone might have recommended that this would be easier, but it wasn't easy, actually. To make a change of this

7

order, a lot was involved. So the women typed, as they might have in the eighties, though it was that awkward decade with no name that came after the nineties.

Despite the shifting technology, the typists had not changed much. They were routinely called girls, though Sylvia was forty-two, Marina thirty-five. They had three children between them. Zero husbands. The older one's hair had streaks of gray at her temples. Her skin had turned down a notch, not blossoming but merely smooth. The younger one's shape had evolved into plushy curviness, or a doughy slouch, depending on how you want to see it. In other ways they might as well have been eighteen or twenty-three, as if they had just woken up to the world of work and been handed an assignment. Beyond the fleetness of their fingers, they were not expected to have expertise or experience to draw on.

Sylvia figured out to pull back the little black latch, and the ribbon settled into its place. They dropped the cassettes into their slots and jiggled them until they sat snug. They sat themselves down and put on their headphones. Marina gave Sylvia a little wave. Sylvia smiled back and then paused as a shadow swept past the opaque glass in the door. The footsteps stopped. A low voice cleared its throat, and then the footsteps resumed. Soon the room filled with the tappity-tapping of the women at their typewriters. Anyone opening the door hours later to ask them if they wanted to order Thai food would have seen the tops of their heads cradled by the bulky headphones. Their eyes would not have flashed up at the speaker until he laughed and did three jumping jacks.

"You want pad thai?" this someone would have had to repeat when Marina and Sylvia pulled their headphones down. Now the instruments circled their necks, the big foam pads pushing up under their chins. Sylvia's face had gone red, Marina's a blotchy pale. They were white women, of a clean, suburban type. They didn't think of themselves as white women because they didn't need to. They didn't see it as an issue or a thing. You can imagine them filling out a questionnaire about their habits, and answering within a very narrow margin exactly like thousands of other women as to the car they drove and the height of heels they preferred.

Marina shook her head at the someone.

Sylvia didn't even look at him.

Ink

The story begins, "They took me into a room and beat me." It goes on, "He cuffed my hands with irons behind my back to the metal of the window and I was hanging there for about 5 hours." It ends, "After careful consideration of this matter, we have demonstrated that . . ." and after that, nothing. The ink with which this final report is printed is called toner. Toner is made of electrostatically sensitive plastic particles, as well as pigment and traces of iron. Toner is safe to ingest in small quantities, though best handled with gloves.

Some inks have ingredients added to make them shine. Without these, words formed on a page look back with utter dullness, brownish black, gloomy, bored and boring. The nice salesgirls in the holiday shop write names on tags with silver and gold ink, creating gleaming curlicues out of words like *Mark* and *Eric*.

Carbon ink remains black, while ink based on gallnuts or tannin-bearing vegetables can turn from green to blue to black and then back again. Lines of choral music or a proclamation about sin start out thunderously dark and then age into a more tentative gray. Some ink chemically incises itself into the page and bonds with the paper, while other ink dries on the surface. We will not judge which is the better ink, because each belongs to its time and category and appropriate situation. Burnt animal bones make boneblack. Mixing this with lampblack provides for a darker combination.

It wasn't even necessary for these so-called detainees to write a statement in blood on the walls. We have extensive accounts, typed out neatly: "They took me into a dark room and started hitting me on the head and stomach and legs. I stayed in this room for 5 days, naked, with no clothes." These narratives, spoken by a translator into a recording machine, made their way from throat to ears to machines, and then back to ears and fingers so that documents with numbers for the detainee, numbers for the document itself, further numbers for the requests and evidentiary procedures, could pass and circulate, or lie in file folders in locked cases in locked rooms. Though some huge percentage of these documents have never been released, you can find PDFs of them online with no trouble. It takes no effort at all to call them up. Just a few of them. Maybe the more palatable ones. There's something definitely handmade about these PDFs, jagged in their margins, crooked from their placement on the copier. The letters are slightly blurred, either from much reproduction or from the ink spray of the original.

I decided to tell a story about two women who typed these accounts.

Typists II

"Hey, Marina?"

Marina kept her head bent, her spine slumped, ears blocked from atmospheric sounds by the heavy headphones.

Sylvia went to the door and flicked the lights. That still didn't do it. Marina's machine represented its passion for duty with a steady clacking and the rhythmic interruption of its end-of-line chime. A French composer created a symphony for such machines, as a kind of musical joke. The pianist Alfred Cortot rebuked his rivals as nothing but "a bunch of typists." These trained boy scouts hit the keys in an orderly fashion, he meant, but music was the ineffable, the cringe and sigh and sudden tearing of the eyes. All that tapping was only a base means of getting there, a necessary interface but not the point.

Sylvia walked up to Marina and placed her hand on her shoulder. Marina flinched, jumping back in her seat. The chair wheels skidded on the carpet. Marina pulled the headphones off her ears. The long cord plopped into her lap, then wriggled to the floor. As all this sudden startled action came to a halt, one last word piped out of the open headphone cup. The women looked away from each other, pretending they hadn't heard.

"I have to pick Jordan up and take him to the dentist," Sylvia said. "I don't know how to report the time."

They looked through some folders, squinting at the poor layout and clunky typeface on the pages of instructions. One printed sheet said it was not necessary to log out and log back in for personal or medical absences of less than two hours; a second implied that any unrecorded absence would be stealing time from the taxpayer.

"Can we ask Georgia?"

Sylvia said she would miss Jordan's appointment altogether if she didn't leave in a few minutes. Marina said she would ask Georgia or Audrey, and then they'd know what to do. In the meantime, Sylvia packed her stuff and got out of there.

When she met her son in the school parking lot, he didn't ask her anything about what she'd been doing at work. She asked him why he was hanging around outside and not in class. The usual system was for her to go to the school office, and then an assistant would go get him.

"Kkk . . . ," he answered, a syllable meaning, What a stupid question. They drove to the dentist in silence. She watched the fish in the fish tank. Afterwards, they went to Popeyes for chicken, his favorite since he was a toddler. She dropped him off at school. She went back to work and typed for two more hours.

Blood

William Harvey discovered the circulation of the blood through a process I've been criticized for describing. Maybe it wasn't necessary to be so precise in the details. Some readers prefer to be spared. Yet we would still think blood only seeped and pooled, rather than raced around the body, if it weren't for Harvey's dogs. He timed the draining of their blood and recorded their whimpers, squirted the entire quantity of blood of one dog into the neck of the next dog, stripped their veins and palpated the valves backwards to figure out the direction of flow. A little terrier picked itself up off the floor and ran around happily, full to bursting with the blood of some lugubrious hound, only to be dissected the next day and the size of its organs examined. The black urine of dogs who had received the blood of other dogs, the jerky actions of their hind legs, the timbre of their howls, and the shape of the instruments involved in these studies, the bladders and membranes, reeds, tubes, and glass balloons—you'll say I'm unreasonable to even bring up this gruesomeness. After all, it was an earlier time. I should appreciate the scientific advances that definitely saved my baby's life hundreds of years later.

The baby and I were just mopping the floodwater out of the furnace room. It comes in through the window well in a hard rain. Clearly he's not a baby anymore, but someone who set up a bed and a table in the basement and sits down there playing his guitar. He's only here for a few weeks. He has his own place, or will as soon as he finds one. The pluckings come up the stairs, notes sounded just for himself but lent to the air. When I'm listening, I'm listening in, overhearing his steady life current.

"When they took me out of the car, a soldier hit me on the face. Then they stripped me naked and made me crawl the hallway until I was bleeding from my chest to my knees," Sylvia typed.

Of course the reader's attention is immediately immersed in the problem of what was on the floor of this hallway and in what way the hallway's surface interacted with the detainee's chest to cause bleeding. I imagine a sheet of blood dripping from below the shoulders, and the head and neck rising free, like a sculptural bust or a headshot on LinkedIn. I won't say I've scoured these documents. Let me not pass myself off as an expert, but rather as someone who has clicked on some links and opened some PDFs and laboriously retyped some sentences, as the format they're provided in isn't copy-pasteable.

Blood can be banked, donated, sold. A line of chairs, each arm draped with the weekly free newspaper, stares out at passing college students from the plasma center on Lake Street. Blood siphoned out of unemployed roofers is fractionated into many wonderful components. The blood of one donor breaks down to platelets, plasma, gamma globulin, albumin, the names exciting to the collector of words. A writer could be writing about anything at all, and steer it towards blood in order to run "clotting factor" over the tongue and indulge in this clusterfuck of fricatives.

The writer relishes the bouquet of consonants. A typist has different concerns. A typist is paid to be accurate. To be loyal to the material. Sylvia transcribed the audio recording, "Then they stripped me naked and made me crawl the hallway," the parts broken down becoming sounds and not words, exhalations and not meanings, a series of keystrokes and not "until I was bleeding from my chest to my knees." A languor set in. The light in the room had hardly changed, but Sylvia's attention had shut down in a late-afternoon way.

"I'm going to pick up the kids," Marina said, embroidering this with an account of her little girl Jayda's after-school activities and the weight of sleepy cutie-pie Gus as she lugged him along in the crook of her arm.

"Yep. See you," Sylvia said. "I'm packing up in a few."

A pile of old napkins and coffee stirrers on top of a filing cabinet moved infinitesimally as the door swung shut behind Marina. Sylvia watched the edges of the paper flutter for a long time.

Audrey

Georgia wasn't sure about the time reports, so she asked Audrey. Audrey didn't know either. She knew how it was in the old system. They decided to call the company headquarters. Georgia was the more experienced and outgoing of the two of them, but that's why Audrey decided to step up and do it. She wanted to appear confident, and to pull her weight.

Georgia hovered over her while she dialed. Audrey spoke clearly to whoever answered the phone. She had to give her ID number, and then answer some questions about her position description. Then she waited. The hold music was exasperating. It seemed to be putting her in a mood of gray tearfulness with its string version of a seventies pop song she couldn't name. A man came on the line. He didn't know squat. He told Audrey to submit a request in writing.

"Sure," she said. "Who do I send that to?"

The man abruptly hung up.

The two of them considered calling the divisional head. That position was vacant still. They didn't know what to do. All they wanted was the most up-to-date time-reporting instructions. The divisional head had an assistant, but that person actually still worked his old job, in another building, as far as they knew. Audrey and Georgia had been rehired for this job, even though they were already doing pretty much the same job. They had had to produce resumes and application letters, though there was no job interview. They underwent extensive background checks, which may not have happened, as no one they knew had said anything about being questioned. They didn't even get a notice—congratulations, you've got the job! One day was the same as the next, except for all the forms they'd had to sign. And who was doing what—it was very confusing. Better than not having a job at all, though, they both agreed.

Georgia told Audrey to forget about it. Audrey went down the hall to the Ladies. She peered at her face. She had little vertical lines cutting through the area between her upper lip and her nose now. Her lipstick seemed to cake up as soon as she put it on. Dry flakes fell out of her eyebrows, and she had to be careful to keep them clean. She wondered whether there was a little brush just for this purpose. She'd never had to worry about this when she was younger.

Nevertheless, with all her concerns about the time reporting, Audrey didn't know what Marina and Sylvia were transcribing in that room.

Netflix

Or some other similar streaming service. In Sylvia's case, possibly the most affordable cable channel. It's a thriller, where a girl is kidnapped not because of the fortune her parents earned in car parts and money laundering but because of her blood's compatibility with the blood of the dying child of some even bigger car parts and money laundering kingpins. All this hinging on a sample of the kidnapped child's umbilical blood, found out from a scan of her adoption records. Then one of the cops on the case turns out to be actually the birth mom of this abducted child. As soon as the kingpin's goons find that out, she's going to be strapped to a gurney and drained.

Consider some fanciful implications: plundering of blood vis-à-vis mining contracts, mineral rights, signing away one's access to one's insides. Menstrual blood leaking becomes a breach. A woman cuts herself opening a can of tuna and is fined $250, a stiff letter from the lawyer insisting she desist this unauthorized bleed.

Years ago I wanted to write a story about something or other, with the subplot gradually coming to the fore of the heroine continually waking up in a bath of menstrual blood. It's happened to me so many times, the sheets absolutely soaked. A slippery sensation disturbing my sleep, and then waking to find myself looking like I'd murdered someone, or been murdered. My first concern is always to strip the mattress and get it all cleaned up. I've even left bloody handprints on the wall, and startled myself with them afterwards. You don't read about that anywhere. This is a story that needs to be told, I thought.

I had the protagonist crossing the ocean on a ship. Her efforts to find out what her employer was hiding in the hold were thwarted by her need to get her own effusions under control. I wrote all I could one weekend when their dad took the kids to his parents' without me, but I stopped when they came back. It was a good story, but it lost its urgency. I haven't looked at it in years. I doubt I'll go back to it anytime soon.

In this thriller about the kidnapping and money laundering, we've also got repeated scenes in a strip club in full swing. These things always want to carry us into places where glamorous women pole dance. I'd almost believe it really is that way in these clubs—youth, strength, sparkly skin.

No matter how hard I try, I can't remember the phrase I came up with for the political science professor portrayed in the thriller as a hunk of flesh. Sylvia wouldn't have worried about it, but just taken it in. I may have written, "The wife of the man collared for drugs is first shown lecturing on Bolshevism to a roomful of undergraduates. By the next scene she's devolved into a sullen lingerie model, standing at the sink in a lace bra and matching tap pants."

That's as far as I can get for now. My question is, what kind of director puts a professor in this getup, though it's probably the choice of dozens of people involved in making the show—the costumer, the designer, the writer, the many editors who checked the screenplay along the way. Surely one of them would have realized that the political science professor's beauty was on the inside. She was only a minor character, but still, one of them could have said something.

Netflix II

Or some other similar streaming service. Sylvia drove home at the end of a workday. She put leftovers in the microwave for her and her son Jordan. He wasn't home yet. She didn't know where he was. It was possible he'd told her he had something after school, but she wasn't listening. It was the biggest argument they had between them, this talking while the other one wasn't paying attention. "I could say anything," she said, and he nodded, meaning he was hearing her say she "could say anything" right now but he wouldn't react or respond or look at her because he was focused on his history homework, of all things. But that was another day. Tonight he wasn't here to not listen. She was equally guilty. He'd probably shouted through the bedroom door that morning where he would be at dinnertime and she answered, "Okay, sweetheart." It meant nothing, Jordan knew. Just a sound. Only if he knocked on the door, came in, and asked her for twenty dollars would she really take note of what he was saying.

She didn't have anything to watch. Marina often told her what she was watching, but Sylvia knew for sure she couldn't stand anything Marina thought was good. She couldn't remember much about what she had watched last. A man, a drug dealer, a strip club. More men, a kidnapping, an averted explosion. An old man, a much younger woman. Pleading. And the much younger woman had given in. The dolled-up forensics student had softened and given the much older detective a promising look. She saw that his heart was kind, even though he was disastrous with people of all sorts. He could storm into the worst junkyard drug den and pull off complicated negotiations, while cab drivers hated him and he had a string of girlfriends pointedly disappointed in him. Nevertheless, the young woman had opened her eyes wide and hesitated. She would give him a chance. Maybe she could be the one to turn him around.

The dolled-up forensics student could do better for herself, Sylvia might have thought if she had remembered that much about the interactions in the last thing she had watched. Sometimes her son played a video game while she pored over a catalog, and the sound of Jordan's character's running feet soothed her. She always asked him to turn the sound down, though that fierce, fake padding of booted feet reassured her.

She could have tried to call Jordan, but it annoyed him when she did that. She checked the calendar in the kitchen, in case the day of the week she'd thought it was all day was actually a different day and he was at show choir practice. She clicked through some selections her streaming service recommended. Who do they think I am? she might have wondered. On the other hand, as far as some of her selections went, they had her pegged.

Ink

Ink stains the writer's hand. Even a wonderful pen like the Pilot Precise V7 can leak as it ages. Little drips of ink in the cap run down the barrel. The writer may look away from the page and notice bluish black spreading all along her index finger and onto the ball of her thumb. Dark marks marble her desk and transfer blotches to her elbows, or to her sleeves. Suppose the writer has stayed up very late making notes. She'll find herself the next morning completely rimed in ink, each nail ringed with it, and a deep blue in the whorls of her fingers that no amount of washing gets rid of. It has to wear off, over days. Suppose she's written, then crossed out, then turned the paper and written up the side margins, and filled in comments between the lines. The ink on her fingers may transfer to below her eyes where she's rubbed them.

Ink on an executive's white shirt is a disaster. The cuffs get dirty gradually, sweat that appears clear and harmless turning the fabric a dusty gray. The executive could pass the shirt on to Goodwill when it reaches this stage. If the executive's shirt encounters ink—still wet on a signature, or bolting from a ballpoint that's come loose at the barrel—this is serious. Unlike sweat stains, an ink stain stands out, exulting in its density. It's a death knell for clothing. The executive could still donate the ink-stained shirt, but the eventual buyer would have to accept it in its ruined state.

The executive may be deciding things all day, approving time sheets, arguing for alignment with strategic priorities, checking over requisitions, rectifying budgets. Laws may be broken or not, depending on how the executive signs or words or deletes or declines certain

Angela Woodward

documents, though generally the consequences won't be felt for many years. Except, of course, for those directly affected.

Clever people have invented many products to eradicate ink from white shirts, such as a white paste a person can paint over the stain. The one tasked with cleaning the shirt in effect puts another stain on top of the original, rather than removing it. Ink stains set in contact with cotton. So do bloodstains. There are remedies, but these spills require quick action.

The writer works slowly. She sits at her laptop and doesn't move a muscle. She'll spend an hour with her chin in her hand, the screen open. She seems restrained by some inner supervisor, even though she's on her own time now, usually very early or very late. She waits, like a servant in a period drama, stiff against the sideboard while the rich folks eat moules marinière. You'd think she was asleep, until the sudden burst of finger movement.

There's more to watch once she's printed out some pages. She crosses out a few words, then rewrites something in the space above the line, which turns out to be more or less exactly the same as the eradicated phrase. She draws arrows on the clean typed draft and scrawls intrusions. She uses an editing symbol called a caret, like a little peaked hat, to mark the spot where other words need to fit into the sentence that needs to fit into the paragraph that she's wrecked already. It gets worse and worse. You'd think she was destroying her manuscript rather than revising it, with all its conflicting markers, this goes there, that must be deleted, and then her comments to herself, *keep this* or *what was I thinking?* or the brackets she uses to mean she needs [something else] there but she doesn't know what it is.

Illegibility

In my pursuit of the uses of ink, I came across the work of Mirtha Dermisache, an Argentinian artist who spent her career crafting book-like creations of illegible scripts. Some of her compositions are drawn in an almost cursive, looking like what's left of a letter long carried in a pocket, or dried out after a flood. It's as if, after a migration of many continents and centuries, the reader no longer recognizes a single letter of the alphabet of her ancestors. Yet it's still familiar. In another of her alphabets, blocks and squares inhabit the pages, assiduously spaced and divided into lines. These inked forms resemble sheets hung out to dry, or buildings on a horizon. The eye focuses on the black shapes, then on the white shapes in between.

Dermisache assembled books, postcards, brochures filled with confident curls, tight black wool arranged with the rhythms and spacings of text. Sentence after sentence of carefully or casually incised squiggles rear up towards meaning, but don't make it. Not in the conventional sense. She invited viewers at her gallery events to sit down with the pages, to pore over them, rearrange them the way they thought best. She allowed anyone to make anything of the lines, the words, the pages. A total freedom of interpretation, where a series of tiny open boxes could mean bread, could mean windows. She seems to have had a real generosity of spirit.

I sat with Dermisache's *Selected Writings* until late last night, poring over ridges like heaps of punctuation, peaked marks like the roofs of tents. Dermisache's letters resembled the tops of letters with the bottom half removed, possibly readable in a mirror or with a special device. A slinky chain of curled squares seemed like the stuffing inside words, a hidden vestibular system the artist had exposed. The sleepier I got, the more it seemed her exuberant scribblings gestured towards a whole nation-state. A library, a town, a network of trade routes, holidays and customs made up a civilization just barely concealed inside this one. She had given a written language to the hissing of the heat vents, the whining of the fridge—living vessels carrying on their own conversations in the background.

The morning broke calmly, the sun replacing the all-night distraction of the streetlights and the neighbor's porch fixtures that took up as soon as I put Dermisache's book down. I didn't think I'd slept at all, but I must have. The even gray sky over the lake urged me towards a benign cheer I wasn't ready for.

The city had to cut down a few of the trees on the main street due to the depredations of the emerald ash borer. It sounds like an enigmatic fortune hunter, but it's a humble bug, making its way north and eating to dust the trees planted along the bigger roads. The ash trees that have gone down this year opened up my view a bit more. The dawn lake spread itself, no ripple on its surface that I could see from this considerable distance. The water offered a pause, an em-dash, an empty parenthesis.

When Monona freezes over, a few weeks from now if it's on schedule, I'll take a walk right out of the park and onto the ice. Towards the middle of the lake, I plan to turn around and see if I can still see my house, pick out through the window a woman sitting at a desk. What is she doing in that quiet place? Her fingers aren't moving. Her eyes are fixed straight ahead.

That woman hardly does anything, I might think. Surely it can't be that difficult, that she squeezes her words out at such long intervals. It's not like she has to invent an alphabet. She trusts in the conventions. She can use the tools that are conveniently lying around—letters, commas, grammatical agreements. She frowns at her screen and then looks up at the wall. She sits and stares. She fidgets, then stills. She leans back in her chair, her cheek in one hand. She stretches her arms up, as if they've gotten sore, then leaves her hands folded on top of her head. She seems to be avoiding touching her keyboard. She stares at the screen, immobile. She's barely breathing. She doesn't look like she's writing at all.

Soap

Sylvia spent a lot of time in the Ladies. She needed to get up and ease her back, and there weren't a lot of places she could go. There was only the tiny break room, with its weak coffee and spray of sugar and sweetener packets, its unwiped table crowned with plastic leftovers containers various workers had left unattended for up to thirty days. A smell crept out of the communal fridge that no box of opened baking soda could countermand. She avoided this place except to microwave a cup of instant oatmeal when she was desperately hungry and not allowing herself Cheetos. A lot of people used this communal kitchen, and someone might come up behind her while she was stirring her oatmeal with a plastic spoon.

"Oh, hi, Lauren," she could say, if she knew the person, but a good portion of the staff had transferred in from elsewhere and declined to specify what they did or where. It wasn't exactly morale-building.

The Ladies had only one stall, and though a second user was welcome to come in and wait by the sink for the first user to finish with the toilet, it was the custom for the second user to wait outside. Otherwise it was too cramped to pass each other by the sink.

Sylvia pumped the soap out of the dispenser into her cupped hand. It seemed to be a new brand, pink and sickly. Its sweetness barely covered a deeper ammoniac sting. It was almost like pee. She rinsed it off and still smelled it. She wondered if a Ladies on another floor would still have the old soap, which was yellow and mild. She vowed to check it out.

Five hours later, she had been back to that same bathroom three times and not once ventured up or down the stairs. Her feet just didn't take her that way. The smell from her hands made her sick. She looked over at the top of Marina's head. The heavy band of headphones crossed her hair, and a bit of forehead didn't disclose her eyes. When Marina suddenly lifted her head, Sylvia was embarrassed to be staring at her. They both took off the headphones, like mirror images of each other.

"What?" Marina said.

Sylvia told Marina about the weird odor of the new soap bugging her, and maybe adding to her persistent headache.

"I didn't notice it," Marina said. "Let me check it out." She took off down the hall. She was gone about ten minutes. Sylvia didn't do anything until Marina came back.

"We could make Alex deal with it. He'd love to take that on," Marina said.

They imagined forcing Alex to get them softer paper towels, too, and what he might say if he wasn't able to change that. Alex was the busybody who trotted in a couple times a day and pretended to be looking for something in the supply cabinet. He had come by that first day with his offer to go in on an order of Thai food. He delivered their completed document folders to someone. He didn't say who. They had no idea what Alex's actual job was.

"I'm bringing my own soap from home tomorrow," Sylvia said. "I just can't stand it."

"Can I use it too?"

"Only you, okay? I'm not bringing soap for the entire building."

"What are you going to get, lavender? We're going to waft it. We'll smell so good, people will follow us down the hall."

"Don't worry," Sylvia said. "I'll just bring in something really normal."

Marina smirked. She seemed unusually chipper today.

Soap II

"What utter enthusiasm in the gift of itself," a poet wrote in an essay called "Soap," admiring the flying streamers, the slobber and froth, as soon as he began washing his hands.

This is not what Sylvia was thinking about. She was occupied by typing, "He took me to the shower and stripped me naked. He said he would come inside and rape me," though the actual rape in this instance was not attested to.

Actually, the French poet Francis Ponge gave up writing his essay on soap. He wrote about rocks, shrimps, candles, always choosing the humble and unnoticed and dedicating his thought and attention to them. The candle drowns itself in its own muck. The mollusk gazes rapt at its nacreous coffin. There's always the hint of violence in his descriptions of the unmoving, the overlooked. Ponge saw the world through things, giving voice to our mute bystanders and witnesses. Though it's more or less unfinished, "Soap" is considered his master-piece. He made lists of what he hoped to write, outlines for further sections, and left them, like the upturned ribs of a boat, right there in the published work. *How little I've accomplished*, he told himself. He wrote with such insight about doors and snails and the baskets berries are packed in, but soap, he said, eluded him.

Ponge passed away long before the era of masculine body washes. He never mused over the square-shouldered bottles in their blues and browns—Every Man Jack, Swagger, Dark Temptation. Ponge composed part of "Soap" in Algeria, funded by a grant. The French literati adored his collapsing stories, their fragile spokes and bubble skins that vanished as soon as the reader turned the page. Every day he walked around the foreign town, staring at the dust on his shoes and remembering aspects of the beast that lived on the edge of his sink back home. Soap is born backwards. It arrives fully formed, and day by day grows smaller and weaker. The scooped sliver curled in the dish has achieved its maturity, all its strength spent. Soap's actions leave no trace, are marked by the absence of marks. Ponge set a few sentences down in his notebook every day, many of them useless, far from capturing what he'd been sent to hunt.

He began the piece during the German occupation of France, when soap was hard to find. He missed it then, and wrote fondly about its eagerness and dedication. It gave itself up foolishly and happily, like a drooling puppy. Ponge worked for the Resistance, spiriting away comrades to safe houses in the guise of his insurance work. He lay low in a little suburb, though he published comic features in the weekly newspaper with tips for better living. He began "Soap" at a time when crimes and their washing away might have been prominent in the minds of many readers.

No matter what Ponge did with "Soap," he couldn't get it right. Camus puzzled over the draft Ponge showed him, and asked for amplifications and clarifications. Ponge also gave the draft to the influential editor Jean Paulhan, who had been his friend and mentor. Paulhan never deigned to respond. He might have been annoyed by it, or he didn't want to hurt Ponge's feelings by telling him his piece was junk. It was easier to say nothing. Maybe Paulhan was just busy.

A few years after this dead end with "Soap," Ponge had acquired a brilliant reputation. Picasso illustrated his poems. Sartre endeavored to explain him. Ponge still hadn't finished "Soap." It lay in fragments, too thin to cohere. He hadn't been able to write it when he was an unknown journalist and insurance man, and now the poet Ponge was about to fail at it, too. In entirely different circumstances he tried again to finish his masterwork, in a peacetime world that revered him.

In Walgreens

Or some other similar chain drugstore. Sylvia was there on a Thursday night with Jordan, but he was one aisle over, pretending he'd come by himself. He had run out of his acne medicine, and he said he couldn't go a day without it. She said she was tired, and she'd pick some up for him tomorrow. His face turned all red. He stayed planted in front of her, looking at his toes, then at her feet propped up on the coffee table. She got up and got her keys.

While he studied the acne ointment and skin care products, she looked at hair dye. It might not be bad to go a little redder. She knew she wouldn't, but she took in the tilt of the model's head, thrown back and sideways so her locks curled over her neck. No one actually looked like that, held their head like that, had hair like that. If they did, no one could help grabbing big fistfuls of it, smelling it, rubbing it against someone's cheek. She put the box back on the shelf and turned away from the alluring glances of similar women, ashy, golden, brown, and raven. Sylvia put her fingers through her hair where it always flattened over her forehead. In the next aisle, earwax softening drops and eye cleansers begged for her notice.

"Mom," Jordan hissed, the syllable stretched into a falling note that signaled reproach bordering on shame. Three shiny steel and navy packages filled his hands. Someone somewhere had designed these paper boxes to be coated with metallic luster and embossed with large numbers in a modern sans serif typestyle. Someone had dictated the curving shape where the silver and navy met and had placed the numerals where they bisected the held-in-check wave. The boxes looked so elegant and knowledgeable and inflexible that the skin the product inside them eventually touched would have to cure itself or be left behind like an undeserving fool. No face would dare have pustules or a greasy sheen when in the presence of the stern creams and serums contained in the boxes her son held.

The price stickers, thoughtlessly jabbed across the brows of these boxes, couldn't be read from where Sylvia stood. Prior experience with this brand told her that each box cost five to seven times what a tube of generic acne medicine cost, and that the trio of boxes comprised a system that couldn't be broken. She would have to buy all three together. This would bring the total price up to or above what she spent on a week of groceries for the two of them. She had previously shown Jordan the list of active ingredients, and told him that it was obvious that the generic tube of benzoyl peroxide and a bottle of witch hazel would act on his skin in the same way as the lofty branded system. "Don't you take chemistry?" she had asked him in this earlier conversation. He had started to cry, not snuffly but eyes brightening and taking a few quick, gasping inhales.

Jordan probably understood from the way she marched to the register that she still felt she was right and he was wrong, but she was going to continue the argument without words, and with the big concession of actually paying for the stuff. In fact the argument was moot as long as she paid. She could be as mad as she liked and he would still have the satisfaction of using this scientifically advanced trio every morning and night for months.

If it was just mother and son involved in the transaction, it would have been okay. The cashier, however, had an opinion too. As the woman in the Walgreens apron passed the vainglorious boxes over the scanner, she brought her eyebrows down. She held the rest of her face perfectly still. She averted her eyes from the shiny boxes and from Sylvia, locking her vision onto a nether plane where she got to decide what was right: only rich snobs would spend so much on their kid's skin, disdaining all the regular people who went without acne systems and much more. The cashier hung in this zone a beat longer than the transaction required. She could see the final price from her perch, but the register's little square was turned away from Sylvia. After letting her silence sink in, the checker announced the total in a monotone, with minimal lip movements.

Sylvia swiped her card through the reader. The machine ejected its flimsy plume of paper. She jerked the pen towards her but had to step closer to the counter, as the writing instrument was constrained by a beaded chain clamped to its rump. She bent over and signed, pressing the paper flat with her other hand. The clerk gestured with the receipt, calling Sylvia's attention to her hand shoving the paper rectangle into the plastic bag. Now the clerk held Sylvia's gaze, the careful emptiness of her expression equaling the dumping of a bucket of disgust. Where she might have said "Have a good evening" or "Thank you for shopping" at Walgreens or some other similar chain drugstore, the clerk merely turned her head towards the man in line behind Sylvia and Jordan.

Sylvia stuck her wallet back in her purse as if burying a corpse beneath a basement subfloor. She scurried for the exit, scarcely having the patience for the sliding doors to react to her body weight and wheel open. She reached back blindly, thrusting the shopping bag at her son. He must have taken it, because she was relieved of it. The bag made crinkling sounds in his lap as they drove home. She turned on the radio. For once, Jordan didn't immediately change the station to his station, and let someone who sounded a lot like Loretta Lynn sing of her sorrows.

Mr. Right

Marina came in smiling and humming, though soon all sound in the room ceased except for the tapping of keys. Sylvia couldn't get comfortable and had to keep shifting her neck and her shoulders. By mid-morning it got to be a physical pain.

"It's the headphones," Marina said. "We really need to get some lighter ones. These have to be from the seventies."

Marina had already said she would talk to Audrey about it. Days had passed, and she must not have. Sylvia didn't want to bug her about it. Whenever she took a break, Sylvia hung the headphones around her neck and dug her fingers into the back of her skull, right where her hair started at her neck.

"They took me to a closed room and poured water on me, and forced me to put my head in someone's urine that was already in that room," Sylvia typed.

Sylvia transcribed a stiff, impersonal voice translating a woe made up of short, simple declarations of injurious actions. Her fingers carried out movements in response to signals they had learned when she was fourteen. Her parents had urged her to enroll in a keyboarding and computer skills class. They had never implied that typing might be her sole means of earning a living, almost from that time forward. She hadn't listened to them about many things, but she had burned to type faster than her next nearest rival. The typing manual was there only to give the girls practice. They could easily have typed chapters from Dickens. Instead of great literature, the typing book had them copy out maxims about punctuality, honesty, and appropriate dress. Its idea of hemlines was way out of date, but the thought behind it, of the clothes not calling attention to the person wearing them, had proved to be long-lasting even when mostly flouted.

Her fingers carried out the quick stabs up, down, this one, that one, that had been drilled into them when Sylvia was in middle school. A tight physical relationship existed between the keys on the keyboard, the letters on those keys, the sounds those letters represented in speech, and the flick and press of index, middle, ring finger. Their endless quick combinations happened as if without thought, just reactions at the speed of thought, the tucking down for the "x," for the comma, the jab to the side for the *g* and *h*. Who knew it could go on for eight hours a day, week after week, that a human's entire life force could be bent into producing these words on this machine.

Marina wanted to make a call around four o'clock. "I think I've finally met Mr. Right," she said. They both laughed, because Marina's men were all so awful. Even knowing this, Marina was unable to resist a certain type who appealed to her kindest nature while ruthlessly stripping her resources. There was the one who had swindled her, and another who had broken her TV and made her pay to replace it. The one she had loved the most had a wife in another state the entire time, though Marina's affairs never lasted more than a few months. Marina said he would interrupt the very nice dinners he took her to to call his wife, smiling at Marina while he said, "Uh huh, uh huh," about the kids and the water heater and their vacation coming up in Cozumel. To her credit, after sitting through this a couple times she had yanked the phone out of his hand and screamed something into it that put a quick end to the shrimp scampi and candlelight.

"Wait," Sylvia said. "Did you talk to Audrey about the headphones?"

"I did, Monday. Didn't she get back to you?"

"I can ask her myself," Sylvia said. "My head is so bad."

Marina said hers was too. They looked at the open boxes on the floor, one by each of their desks. They hadn't even made a dent in the mound of mini cassette tapes. These boxes represented a lot of paychecks.

Marina went to a good cell phone spot down the hall to call her latest Brett or Miles or Justin. Someone walking by might have heard her laughing and saying, "You bet. Yep. Can't wait. See ya," but Sylvia wasn't in on it.

Sylvia didn't do anything until Marina came back. In that interval, she kept the headphones on, and her foot rested on its heel, the ball just over the pedal that operated the Dictaphone. Her wrists held steady at the level that would let her fingers drop easily onto the keys. Her elbows splayed out, making a vee of her arms. Her eyes focused on a white space on the page, just below the last line she had typed. It was as if nothing had happened yet, and nothing was about to happen. When the door clicked and pushed its rectangle across the entryway, she started up again.

The Material II

My mother called to bug me again about coming for Thanksgiving. My daughter had already signed herself up. It was only a two-hour drive for her. My mother dangled my daughter like a lure, knowing I'd end up sitting on the sofa with her, holding her arm and laughing about something from fifteen years ago.

"I'm sorry. But I already told you," I said. "I need the time to myself."

"Don't you live alone?" she countered.

Before noon even on Thanksgiving, my younger sister's two boys had pummeled each other, and one had to be sent out to the car. We argued about who had to sit in the chair next to the broken table leg, which had once given way. No one trusted the repair that had been done. My brother's little girl got underneath and described the strips of metal bolted into the table's underside. "But it still might fall," my brother said to her. He shook the table to make it wobble. That made her cry for most of the rest of the meal.

Nobody said anything to me, except to tell me how great my daughter looked and how proud they were of her. Everyone maintained that she was smart and pretty. I almost thought I was going to move among them as nothing more than the woman who'd brought up that wonderful child. Then Delia volunteered me to tell them about my visit to the office supply store. We had draped ourselves over the love seats in the living room, digesting. My mother and Dennis were in the kitchen, washing up. "No, sweetie," I said. "I don't think so." So she began telling her aunts and uncles herself about what I had told her, and only her. "You know she's working on this book about the detainees at Abu Ghraib," she said.

"No, darling," I said. "They don't want to hear this."

She launched into it anyway, paying me back for the times I told embarrassing stories about when she was little. How she had pretended to be a moth when she was three, and thought dogs were small horses. "Mom was in this office supply store," she said, leaving out that it was an ancient, almost bankrupt place that hadn't changed much since the eighties. It had made me almost sick with joy when I crossed the threshold. I inhaled the dusty perfume of the narrow aisles and took in the stacks of graph paper notebooks and boxes of Corrasable Bond. I'd been drawn to the pen rack, where they had a full line of German engineering pens of varying widths. They had replacement ink cartridges for them, too. My face flushed. This place was a gold mine.

"And so she wrote on the little paper pads," my daughter said, "to try the pens out, this stuff she has memorized. She tested all the pens, writing what they said in evidence, you know, 'They took me into a room and beat me. They made me crawl down the hallway.'"

Delia had missed the last time my writing project came up during the holidays. She'd been at her dad's, and I hadn't briefed her afterwards except to say there was the usual tragedy. Without removing my gaze from my knees, I could tell that my siblings' faces were locked into disapproving grimaces. A clanking in the background must have been my brother looking for more beer. He didn't need to repeat the scene from a few years ago, when he'd shouted at me that I shouldn't keep on writing about this when the culprits were in jail already. Stabbing search phrases into his tablet and waving news stories at me, he said that it was all over. "Nobody wants to hear this stuff," he said.

Correct. But that was the whole point.

I maintain that he hit me on the chin with his iPad, but my siblings all swore I had stepped into it. And it wasn't like he'd knocked a tooth out, anyway. They considered me a baby for being upset about it.

Delia described the proprietor of the office supply store putting his hand on my hand after I completed my purchase of three pens and six ink refills. "'If you need any help . . . ,' he said," she said.

I had thought I looked so shabby that he was offering me a job. Then, realizing what had happened, I spat back, "It's not me who needs help!" Somehow I had imagined the store proprietor could call up the beaten men with me from their simple accounting of what had been done to them. Especially at that time, their story was everywhere. You could hardly not know. That was my error. Before Delia could bring me to life, standing outraged and fuming in the face of this kind old man, my sister Katie stood up and declared it was time for the kids to go to bed.

"I'm not a kid!" my daughter said.

All her aunts and uncles looked down at the carpet. Delia looked genuinely bewildered.

Alex

Sylvia and Marina weren't sure what Alex did. It wasn't polite to ask, or if you'd already asked two or three times and didn't get it or couldn't remember, it seemed rude to ask again. He kept the copiers running, or called the company the copiers had been leased from if it was beyond what he could do. He filled the paper trays, made sure Marina and Sylvia had enough blank forms, and took their finished folders down the hall. He also sometimes organized the plastic stirrers in the coffee room, picking up all the unused strays and putting them in the glass jar without a lid, upright. These little chores couldn't take forty hours a week. Marina told Sylvia that she'd complained to one of their coworkers that she couldn't find the sweetener in between all the sugar, and later she walked past the break room and saw Alex with the little sugar packet bin on the table, sorting.

"Word got round," Sylvia said.

Their theory was that he was keeping track of them. They laughed about it, making devious expressions at each other behind his back whenever he came in to pick through the supply closet. Fact was, there was another supply closet. No reason any of that stuff needed to be kept in the typists' room.

The waft of air as Alex came in brought both of them to a halt. Sylvia watched his eager elbows as he bent down to look through the shelf of rubber band boxes.

The plain, unscented soap in a pump bottle Sylvia had left on the sink of the Ladies had disappeared after three days. Marina had asked Alex about the new brand of soap once already, shaking her fingers under his nose. "We can't use this stuff," she said. "You have to fix this."

Marina and Sylvia had laughed about his expression, which was a complex mixture of surprise, woe, and determination. They couldn't have laid odds on whether he would manage to change the soap in the Ladies back to the old brand or not.

Marina took off her headphones. "What about our soap, Alex?"

"I'm looking into it," he said. "I'll let you know. Don't worry about it."

Marina told him that Sylvia had brought her own soap, and someone had snatched it.

"I'm sorry to hear that," he said. "That's not right."

"Well, get on it," Marina said. "A crime's been committed."

Sylvia didn't say anything. She let her hands take a rest on her lap. It was much harder work typing than keying on a computer keyboard.

Alex exited quickly. He didn't take any rubber bands with him. Marina gave Sylvia a level look. Sylvia pretended to type, but she was just pressing the space bar with one finger. She kept the headphones on. They made a kind of hissing, sucking sound in her ears, even when she didn't depress the foot pedal and release sound. She heard that background fizz now as she lay in bed at night. It seemed to float underneath any other sound of speech or television.

She looked up again, and Marina's mouth was moving. Her eyes crinkled up in a laugh. The sound in Sylvia's ears was like the back of a throat in a heavy breath, a precursor to a cough or a clearing "ahem." The heavy exhale never reached an endpoint and a reversing inhale. It just went on, louder and softer, filling gaps on the tape, and then receding as the voice took up: "They left me hang from the bed and after a little while I lost consciousness. When I woke up I found myself still hang between the bed and the door."

"What did you say?" she shouted to Marina. They each lifted one ear cup off one ear.

"Job skills are people skills," Marina said. This was a phrase their prior boss used to say, to explain how certain obscure personnel decisions were made. And he had moved way up the ladder, especially after hiring someone to write his application letters for him.

"Yeah, right," Sylvia did not hear herself say, as the heavy plastic and foam encircled her ear. She pressed the space bar a bunch more times. She began to calculate how much money she would have left after her rent and utilities were paid. The night that her son hadn't come home until nine, he had been at his show choir's travel meeting. Show choir was considered "for girls," but the music teacher had begged Jordan to try out. They were going to perform at Disneyland, after, of course, they raised enough money through weekend car washes. Sylvia suspected that the car washes would offset the cost of the bus trip by a couple hundred dollars at most, and she would be left to pay for four nights of hotel, all meals, event tickets, and various other expenses that the choir director didn't dare spell out.

Soap III

Anything that's not soap would tell us about soap. Its job is the removal of grapplers from surfaces, its more generic name being surfactant, the loosener. The grasp on the baton relaxes. The stain on the pants leg flows away. Dirt and dust, transferred from the ground to the skin, release their hold. Soap uncouples, taking any tight situation and solving it with slick slipperiness, sliming away unwanted particles. The scaly material that clings to the hand and the arm, to the uniform or the chair or the rug, agrees to go away when soap intervenes. Just the other day I turned away and got in the car, too overcome to give a last look when my son took off again for Colorado. His time in my basement was just a stopover between leases. I find these partings unbearable, while soap manufactures goodbyes every day, escorting without remorse the dearest bits of someone down the drain.

"He took me to the shower and stripped me naked. He said he would come inside and rape me," Sylvia typed, this phrase dragging her attention yet again to soap. We can see soap in two camps, in one the hard yellow bar, stinking of disinfectant, belonging to school washrooms and farmyard troughs, anywhere the promise of cleanliness can be distorted into a punishment. In the other, the gardenia and lilac that smooths the skin as it cleanses, that adds value, you could say, by softening, pleasing, perfuming, turning a body washed into an angel almost. The word *soap* is as duplicitous as *dog*. Some breeds of dogs are tall and square jawed, others roly-poly fluff balls—it's not fair that they all get to be combined under one noun.

The poet Ponge returned to his essay "Soap" again and again. The finished document seems flagrantly aimless, full of repetitions, as if he's just moved the pieces around, or revved himself up for a running start by writing all over again one paragraph he was satisfied with. He compares soap's bubbles to bunches of grapes, a terribly inapt figuration. Sensing how wrong the comparison is, he nevertheless stubbornly repeats it. He says that when soap is used up, it's like a person with bags under their eyes, who has "had it." The translator props up "had it" inside scare quotes, making the French expression stumble into English on crutches. The reader encounters this injured creature multiple times. Ponge's ugly phrasings hang around like awkward party guests, heavy handed, unsure, and persistent. Ponge compares "Soap" to his other poems and concludes that his only successful ones were the ones he barely worked on.

Ponge left Camus's letter critiquing "Soap" right in the published version of the essay, along with his many notes to himself, the goals he set and didn't meet, his calendar and expectations. He found himself to be writing about what he couldn't write about. "Wasn't there something?" he writes, referring to the wartime years when he began the piece. Soap is ecstatic, it revels in itself, snatching at the air. He includes in the essay a diary entry where he writes that he'll destroy the draft of "Soap" entirely on August 15th.

Soap foams. It exults. It has much to say. And then it stops speaking. Ponge began the piece in 1941, and declared it almost sort of finished in the sixties, when he might have forgotten entirely his wartime deprivations and work in the Resistance. He seems to have washed himself away in the process of writing, expunging himself in his celebration of the foolish mutterings of the slippery stone. Ellipses and parentheses carpet the essay, showing how much has been cast aside, not followed up, or corralled into polite mumbling. Wasn't there something? he asks himself towards the end of the piece, some reminiscence that sparked his enthusiasm for soap? One of his critics claimed Ponge created a "deafening silence" over the crimes the earlier, wartime Ponge might have been laboring to expose in his little ditty.

described being taken to the shower, stripped naked, and
    told he would be raped
might conclude that soap here was used or threatened to be
    used as a lubricant
soap's relationship with nudity something Ponge never
    touched on, its intimacy with bare skin

I wonder if scouring powder gets to be included in a chapter on soap, whether it's also considered a soap, as is detergent. I might get myself off course if I go for the whole set of materials dedicated to the removal of other materials, like bleach, Ajax, and OxiClean. The eraser, the redactor, the censor, the ones who lose documents and delete files, might also come under this category.

I'm probably just as pathetic as Ponge in my trepidations and false starts. I can hardly bring this story forward, though I've been thinking about it for years. I step aside, apply myself to something else, return to find nothing changed. "Needs connection," my notes to myself say. Last month I carried a few pages of the previous chapter around in my handbag until they got creased and smeared. I read them through on the bus, then put them back again. Once I jabbed the pen right through the paper when the passenger next to me knocked my elbow with her backpack. "Oh, sorry," she said. "I hope I didn't ruin it."

Eventually I tossed the pages into the recycling. I may or may not have made the changes I promised myself. Still, Ponge gets to us by being so vulnerable. He's such a convincing failure. Ponge can't help being painfully aware of not saying what he wants to say. He blathers away, then trails off. That's what "Soap" is all about, then: silence.

Ice II

I got sick after Christmas and spent four days in bed. The last time I was out, I'd walked up along the edge of the lake in a gray mist, thinking the water would never freeze. It chopped around, barely visible below me but obviously in violent movement. It muttered against the rocks, a restive, repetitive cursing. That night I threw up and went through the rest of whatever stomach flu I came down with. I rested my cheek on the rim of the toilet and fell asleep for a few minutes, kneeling. What should have been my vacation days went to recuperation, blinds drawn, drinking broth. With this week obliterated, I missed the transition when the lake at last settled into its stubborn sheet of solidity.

I like to choose my seat on the bus to work so that I can see the lake as we go along it. It peeks out between structures, though the whole landscape can be blotted out by people standing in the aisle, or even just sitting in the opposite seats in a particularly broad-shouldered way. I try not to read, but to look out, or study my hands. This morning I got absorbed in the conversation of two women behind me. I couldn't believe how much they revealed, knowing they were ringed with perceptive strangers. They were obviously good friends who nevertheless didn't see each other often. The first one talked about going quail hunting with her husband, and some other travel, to Oregon and maybe Mexico, over their brief holiday break. They'd been to desert and forest and someplace they could swim, and just got back two days ago. The other woman talked about inviting her parents-in-law over for lasagna, and they didn't show up. It turned out the old people were waiting for the young people to come to their house. So she and her husband packed up the toddler and the baby and the huge pan of lasagna, and on top of it had to apologize for being late. She was sure, she said, that the invitation was the other way around, but she was too polite to his parents to insist.

The two women laughed about this, then the one who had gone quail hunting told the other one that she had big news that she'd been keeping back. She and her husband were splitting up. "The feeling is gone," she said. He was depressed all the time and didn't see the use of bringing another child into such a world. This didn't really match the whole quail-hunting story she had just told.

"What? I can't believe it," the lasagna woman said. "I'm so sorry."

"Nothing to be sorry for," the other woman said. "I'm fine. I feel absolutely nothing."

"That might be kind of a defense, but I know what you mean," said the second woman.

All around them, people stared into their phones or listened to podcasts on earbuds. No one acknowledged the conversation. All those who must have overheard gave the impression of being absorbed in their own entertainment. I looked down at my lunch bag on my lap, pretending I hadn't eavesdropped, though I managed a quick glance.

The consoling woman's face looked stricken. She clenched her teeth, holding a benign smile over a bleak expression. The one whose marriage was suddenly over stared ahead, serenely blank.

The History of Ink

Though soap touches our story, and ice, blood, urine, and some other things, I continue to fixate on ink, that humble, unnoticed conveyor of thoughts and ideas, words and sounds. I'd been looking for a long time for a book called simply *The History of Ink.* The public library waited months before telling me it had lost its copy. It was an old book, and no other libraries would send it over to mine. Then it turned out to be easy to find it on Amazon or another similar online purveyor. I had it overnighted, and it arrived this afternoon, just in time to delay my telling of Marina's encounter with Mr. Right.

The book was printed only yesterday, and there isn't any other date on the inside cover. I figured out that it's a soft-cover facsimile of the original, a volume from 1857. I'm amazed to find the author has elaborated on many of the facets of ink that interest me too: the way it incises the paper, the formulas that allow ink to grow darker over time versus the inferior vegetal concoctions that go the reverse route, from blue to green to barely legible yellow. This author also rails against paper and the part it plays in how well or how poorly ink survives. He wishes paper would take responsibility for its role in ink's story. He finds any claims from China to have invented a superior ink thousands of years ago to be entirely spurious. The Chinese, he says, latched onto documents European traders brought them much more recently. Then they faked manuscripts to give themselves a proud history. This author also derides the Chinese for painting with fine animal-hair brushes. True ink, he says, must flow through a tube, such as a reed or quill. If it gets glopped up in the passage from hollow container to the page, it can't count as a good ink. Those who brush ink onto cloth are cheating. They're not writing at all.

This author gave the recipe for an inferior ink, to prevent good people from being ripped off by peddlers who ask too much for this crap. "Now for the price of this book you can make your own ink," he wrote. He also said flat out that this low-quality ink might be good enough for Americans and Australians. I took that blow without too much rancor. The biggest impact on me was this author's use of the words STAIN and TINT in all caps, which I interpret as SHOUTING.

Thank goodness I bought that book, because now I know about a predecessor of writing ink, "shoe ink," which cobblers coated on their leather. This substance was in everyday use for ages before anyone thought to brush it on the wooden dies used to print playing cards. It took another leap from printing the playing cards to using ink to manufacture placards and announcements, but words are much less interesting than either boots or gambling. I have many more questions about the cotton tape, folded into thirds and soaked in ink, used by the sturdy typewriter Smith-Corona. For that I have to chase down another couple books at the state historical society.

Sylvia and Marina typed their documents on that fantastic machine the IBM Selectric. The Selectric used plastic tapes in place of cloth ribbon, and placed the letters on a rotating ball rather than on keys like a piano. The ink was not soaked into the ribbon but sprayed on electrostatically. The old-fashioned cotton ribbon needs to recuperate from the ordeal of having printed a letter. A metal baton has punched it in the gut and forced all its ink to flow onto the page, which acts like a hospital bed beneath it. The remaining ink on the ribbon quickly flows towards the injured place and refills the gap. Very soon, maybe even only microseconds later, the ribbon is again prepared to take the blow. It has a kind of solidarity with itself, even as it's flailed on, blow after blow, probably by the sweetest and most unassuming lady typist.

The Selectric's polymer tape abandoned its ink to the paper entirely. With each impact of the key, the ink peeled off and fled all the way to the other team. The tape was eventually left with a precise record in white on black of all that had been typed on it. Later models improved the motion of the tape so that strike after strike of the key landed in almost the same place, obscuring this reversed record. Still, supervisors of girl typists, lady typists, or young men were advised to collect the used tape cartridges and dispose of them carefully in order to "avoid unintended disclosure."

The Selectric was known for its "great uniformity of character shape," due to its complete and total shedding of its pigment onto the paper. Its ink did not

> rub off on the typist's hand
> its typed product withstands handling
> and is relatively fade-proof in sunlight
> "uncuffed us and then he punch us in the stomach and hit
>   us on the face"

one of the girls typed.

At the end of each day, Alex came by and took Marina's and Sylvia's folders full of typed sheets, which by the way were not vague white pages but triplicate forms labeled with the name of the interviewee, the location including address, a file number, and a number for the interviewee.

Sylvia and Marina fell historically into the era just before the ubiquity of fillable PDFs. The three-colored carbonless forms had established routing, signature, and filing routines that hadn't yet been reimagined. Sylvia and Marina thought they were unfortunate to get stuck in a typewriter job because of all the annoyance of the correcting tape and correction fluid. At the same time, they considered themselves fortunate to be employed, and it wasn't worth looking much deeper than that. If Alex collected their used-up tape cartridges, they hadn't been told about it.

Angela Woodward

Here's a bit from a poem by Lord Byron, but I don't know which one yet:

> But words are things: and a small drop of INK,
> Falling like dew upon a thought, produces
> That which makes thousands (perhaps millions) think.

Marina's Date

"I don't want to talk about it," she said, which relieved Sylvia of remembering what Marina was referring to. Marina was wearing over-the-knee heeled boots. These violated the dress code that they had both signed off on. In principle they would have followed it without a contract and system of warnings for violation, since it was clear to the women that conformity was highly valued in the workplace. They noted what others wore in terms of bracelets and colors and bows on blouses, and followed suit. They saw nothing wrong with this. All in all, it made things easier.

Marina might have remembered the cleaner who had gotten fired. Like most of the cleaning staff, she was Hispanic, but she was not a stooped grandma but a gorgeous mama. She came to work in tight, shiny blouses, little skirts, high heels. She put the drab blue wrapper on top, but it didn't totally disguise her. Don told Audrey to tell this woman to knock it off. Apparently there was a big flap about it. She looked like a model, Audrey said. Lord knows why she was working here. She had had to be terminated. Marina wouldn't dream of dressing like that, though she had a rebellious streak.

Sylvia put the headphones on. A voice filled her ears. "He hit me hard on my chest and cuffed my hand to the window of the room about 5 hours and did not give me any food that day." Her fingers skittered over the keyboard. The typewriter clacked and clanged. Sylvia's posture degraded bit by bit, even though she tried to remember. Her lower back ached, and it seemed like she couldn't get her shoulders to straighten.

"I don't know if I'll see him again or not," Marina said later. "After everything was so wonderful. I thought he was great. I don't know. He really seemed like Mr. Right."

Now Sylvia remembered. Anyone else but Marina could have chosen a man for Marina. Her instinct for the wrong ones was unfailing. Sylvia rubbed her temples and put her hands to the back of her neck. They had both taken a little break at the same time, which was why Marina was giving her the scoop.

"Do you think he meant it?" Marina asked, after having told Sylvia in much more detail than she wanted to know about Marina's date quietly watching TV while she put her kids Gus and Jayda to bed. Then they kissed for a little while, the first time. Then he ordered her on her knees to suck him off, and just before he came he grabbed her up and bent her over the arm of the couch. "He was really rough" was mercifully all that went into describing the next series of actions. He had called her "bitch" in her ear while he did it.

"Maybe it's just a game. The thing is, afterwards he was completely normal and calm. Sweet, really. Peaceful. I don't know what to think."

Sylvia didn't have any kind of answer. "Wow," she said.

"He's so cute," Marina said.

"The kids stayed asleep?"

"The door was open a crack. Jayda needs the light in the hall. I don't know. I think so. I assume so. They sleep pretty soundly."

"Wow," Sylvia said. She had no choice but to converse with Marina. They were in this together. They really liked each other, too. But it might have been nice if she didn't have to know absolutely everything.

"Great boots," she said.

"Little pick-me-up," Marina answered. "They hurt my toes, though."

Show Choir Costume

Sylvia didn't know anything about it, but Jordan insisted he had given her a form and she had filled it out and signed it.

"You know you did!" he insisted, and she held back her snippy or mocking reply in the face of what seemed like more than the usual temper.

"Jordan," she said.

He blew out his lips, a big sighing breath she recognized as a habit of hers. His face had gotten all red. She always encouraged him about his complexion and said his acne wasn't at all noticeable, that no one cared but him, but she felt alarmed and sorry for him at the big welt on his cheek and the crowd of dots across his forehead. She clamped down her pity before it escaped, but Jordan caught the whiff of it. This was enough to turn the tide against her.

The amount he needed for his show choir costume was more than two car payments. She didn't see how this could be right. She then irritated Jordan further by asking him to describe the costume in detail, and asking if he had an itemized sheet or form or something that said how much the vest and pants and jacket cost separately.

"That's not the point!" he said.

Sylvia moved across the kitchen to get out of the way of his intense gaze. Her retreat opened up a line for Jordan to the fridge. He took the Fritos off the basket on top and walked to the couch with the bag. She followed and stood over him while he hunched, spraying crumbs, eyes locked on the blank black screen.

"Jordie, we'll make it work. I don't like to be surprised by an expense like this, that's all."

The Fritos bag received all Jordan's wounded mournfulness. His shoulders looked frail, and his neck had adorned itself with an Adam's apple way too big for it. The one blazing pimple on his cheek seemed to dare her to look at it, rather than at her son as an entire suffering being. The red volcano manifested Jordan's feeling that every single thing his mother did was unfair, because of the custody arrangement with his dad that he had no say in. There was a ton Jordan didn't know about that. She'd only ever given him the most sanitized version. In fact his dad, as Sylvia described him to Jordan, was an ethical, blameless character whose hands had been tied by fate. Her tirades—"You're so selfish! Think of Jordan! Think of him!"—had occurred in parked cars or over the phone when Jordan was at school or once behind the bleachers at a soccer game, when Jordan's dad had still lived somewhat near their school district, and with only one of his three subsequent kids. The only way she could disabuse Jordan of his sense of her own selfishness in keeping him to herself would be to remind him of how he had looked coming back from his last vacation visit to his dad's house. The idea of calling her ex and asking him to pay half the show choir costume appeared only in the same fantasy that Jordan had: Dad was bound by sad but immovable edicts not to give Jordan an allowance or buy him clothes or help out with any school expenses.

Sylvia told Jordan to find a copy of that form she had filled out. He answered by chewing the Fritos louder. She softened to the "honey, sweetie" approach, seeing him as he'd been only a few years earlier, a cute, big-headed child. The hand diving into the bag slowed. She watched Jordan's wrist suspended in the mouth of the foil package. She inched closer to him on the couch. The hand dropped down and came up with a revolting mass of chips. Jordan got himself into a rhythm, grabbing and chewing, not looking at the bag, his mother, or his hand. This automaton managed to ring itself with Fritos crumbs. Rather than reaching towards him to start sweeping them off the upholstery, Sylvia launched herself out of the room.

The old, barely working kitchen laptop couldn't seem to connect to the school's online portal. She closed the machine and put some water on for noodles. While it came to a boil, she leaned against the stove. The chomping in the next room slowed to a more intermittent pattern. When the water bubbled, she let it go on without tending to it. Its sound gradually turned into the hissing of the cassette tapes at work. The water making its tumult almost seemed like an introduction to one of those phrases, "They made me crawl the hallway until I was bleeding from my chest to my knees." Or the boiling could have been the sound that came after the voice stopped speaking. The blank tape, the waiting. In the ten minutes or so Sylvia had been arguing with Jordan about the show choir costume, she had forgotten about that sound. It hadn't gone away, just been pressed under briefly.

Urine

One day a poet got a grant to go to Algeria to write, and came up with nothing. He looked out his window at a man and woman walking down a path. The man walked three paces ahead of the woman, and both their heads were bowed. "Make a poem out of that," the poet thought, but the next time he looked up, the path was empty. A donkey cart came the other way. "That's the cutest thing ever," thought the poet. No way anyone was making a poem out of it. It would be good to have someplace to start, but there really wasn't one.

The poet met some friends from Paris in the bigger town. After the long bus trip, they ordered some wine in the restaurant attached to the hotel. "You wouldn't believe what we heard," said Evangeline. The poet felt his heart rate pick up. He knew that whatever Evangeline told him, he'd manage to make into a poem. Franz interrupted her, and before too long they were fighting about their daughter. Evangeline hated the daughter's boyfriend, and Franz said she had no right to interfere. The air seethed between them. The poet thought that the boyfriend was a stand-in for Franz himself, that something that Evangeline didn't like about the boyfriend was a criticism of Franz. Everyone knew he had cheated on Evangeline for years, with a plain, boring schoolteacher. Luckily the teacher was married too, and she cut Franz off without a word after something happened one Easter. The way all their friends had avoided telling Evangeline any of this had created a white space of omission. When the poet ran into Franz and his mistress at a movie, he had to recount it later as that Franz was alone. "You never told me you saw that!" Evangeline said. The poet thought of Evangeline as a mummy, swathed in soft streamers of fabrication.

The poet concentrated on Franz's throat, dotted with stubble and interrupted by bulky tendons. This fleshy column rippled as he took a drink. The head above, the shoulders below, vanished into insignificance. The set of tubes encased in prickly, sunburned skin gulped wine and forced air up for the evasions that came out of Franz's mouth. "She loves him," the mouth said, the pouchy skin on either side of the Adam's apple contracting and loosening.

What Franz really meant was, his daughter was happy being a dupe of this chilly person she'd started living with, and Evangeline would never bring herself to confront Franz with what she surely knew about the affair with the teacher. "You want to be so stupid," Franz implied. The muscles of his neck obligingly created the conditions for this sneer.

"All I'm saying," Evangeline said. The poet tried not to listen. He wanted her to tell him about a traveler she'd met, who had survived in the desert by drinking turtle urine.

"How did he get the urine?" the poet would have asked her.

Evangeline would have told him the method. If you pick it up, it pees as a defense mechanism, pouring its lifesaving balm into the traveler's palm. The traveler had managed ten days in the desert with only this to keep him going.

The poet had an idea that nouns could be rocks, and verbs, water. The verbs slither past the rocks, pound them, erode them gradually over millennia, go after them with hammers, pierce them with arrows. Nouns lie dead and buried, but also find themselves sitting upright in rocking chairs, or presiding over alpine fields. What the rocks mean might be arbitrary, or shift over time, but nevertheless the verbs are relentless, flowing, scraping, perforating, abrading with all the force imbued in them by their creator. Adjectives wander onto the scene, sunny peacemakers, living in the moment, it will all be okay.

Evangeline huffed out a long breath, meaning she was so exasperated she wasn't going to say anything more. The meaty stalk Franz's head hung on swiveled slightly, allowing Franz to smile while turned away from his wife. His lifelong victory over her was assured.

The waiter came back, speaking the rough, accented French he had studied in school. After he finished his speech, he made his face into a shield, and hid behind it his loathing of them, and his boredom, and his satisfaction with having a regular wage that allowed him to support not only his own children but the children of his two brothers. Of course, he might have been thinking anything, and even in creating this loathing for him, the poet was falling further into the trap of imperialism. Only that turtle urine might have escaped the rake of politics and culture. No, that too is implicated in the disaster of human civilization, the poet thought. Tuning out Evangeline entirely, he listened to the insistent laughter from the surrounding tables, men chuckling and snorting, sweet, high feminine ha-ha-ha's raining down amid the tinkle of forks against dessert plates.

Mr. Right Has a Name

"What utter enthusiasm in the gift of itself," the French poet Ponge wrote in his essay on soap, admiring the flying streamers, the slobber and drool that let loose as soon as he began washing his hands. "They took me to a closed room and poured water on me, and forced me to put my head in someone's urine that was already in that room," Sylvia typed, as the words spoke themselves into her headphones. The voice was not the voice of the person whose experience was being recorded. He was a translator. He might have had special training in keeping his voice dispassionate. He was after all only a vessel for the language of others. The passionate one in the room that day was Marina.

"I can't eat," she said. Marina's nerves were strung out because she was seeing Mr. Right again that evening. He was coming by at eight, after the kids were asleep. She thought they might really be able to talk, with some hours to themselves. She thought he maybe had something to say to her.

Sylvia wondered if Mr. Right's information was that he was married, like that other one of Marina's more financially stable lovers. But of course, if he was married, that was the last thing he would reveal. She thought Marina might have figured out by now that she had to ask her disastrous men directly about their employment history, indebtedness, and marital status.

Marina skipped lunch due to her tension, or because she had no food in the house due to her previous engagement with Mr. Right on what would have been her grocery shopping night. She went down to the vending machine and came back with Cheetos, or some other similar salty, crunchy junk food. The room filled with the odor of fake cheese, as well as with the relentless tapping of typewriter keys.

Sylvia neared the end of one of the cassettes. "They took me to a closed room," she typed, "and poured water on me, and forced me . . ." The typewriter seemed all het up, zinging with proficiency. Her ankle ached from pressing the treadle that started and stopped the dictation machine. Her ears sweated, encased in the heavy headphones. The air in the room did not circulate unless someone swished the door open, and that would only be Alex with his Thai food, or to get toner out of the supply closet. The rest of the building used regular word processors and printers, though of an out-of-date, clunky, beige kind that would one day wring nostalgia out of viewers of a movie set in the era in which these ugly machines had been manufactured. Sylvia concentrated on the dwindling diameter of the tape on the left-hand spindle. The other spindle thickened, but it was the diminishing one that meant something to her. Not that there weren't a seemingly endless number of tapes left in the box, but coming to the end of one was still a point in time that differed from the surrounding ones.

"They took me to a closed room and poured water on me," she typed, "and forced me to put my head . . ." She hadn't gotten around to doing laundry last night. That's because she had run out of Cheer a week ago, and she'd forgotten to get more when she was last at the store. One of these days her son was going to learn to do his own laundry. It was ridiculous that she still did it for him.

Marina sat unmoving at her machine. She had pushed the headphones down around her neck. Her bangs clung to her forehead in a sticky mat. A little pile of wadded napkins ringed her elbow. Her face had fallen. Every feature that could go down had drawn down, her eyebrows low, her cheeks flat and slack, her mouth slightly open in a a frowning grimace. This desolate face stared at the dead air between the two desks.

Although Marina was the younger of the two women, she held her expression as if practicing for the wreck gravity might make of her years from now. Sylvia watched her, while also watching the tape continue to unwind. It looked like it had to be at the very end, the pause would come soon, but the material continued to feed itself onto the other spindle. "He took me into the shower," she typed.

"Marina," she called across the desk, while her fingers kept on typing. She couldn't hear her own voice with the headphones on. "He took me to the shower and stripped me naked. He said he would come inside and rape me," she typed. A tiny distant sound was her asking Marina if she was okay.

As if a button had been pressed, Marina animated her face, smiling and tucking back her hair. "Just thinking about Ted," she said. "I can't get him out of my mind."

That's terrible, Sylvia wanted to say. I can't believe you'll see that guy again. From the little she'd been forced to listen to about Mr. Right, he was an even worse chump than the others. Is Ted the guy who shoved you to the floor to suck him off? she felt like asking. The one who called you "bitch" in your ear, then acted like nothing had happened?

Sylvia didn't ask, because that was surely who Marina was referring to. More of his story would be pretty hard to take.

Marina clamped her headphones back on, exiting the frozen anguish she had unwittingly broadcast. The room stank of Cheetos, and another, deeper staleness. Bits of orange cheese powder rimmed the inside of her lower lip. Her eyes shone.

Netflix III

Or some other similar streaming service. Sylvia and Jordan used to like to watch those compilation shows together where pets did funny things and old women fell backwards into pools at weddings. They had continued a Sunday-night tradition of immersion in other families' lives even when Jordan seemed too old for it and Sylvia was embarrassed by how crass and sometimes cruel it was. But now they rarely watched network TV, and if that show was still on, they didn't tune in. Tonight Jordan was at his friend Parrish's house. Sylvia idly clicked through her streaming service's suggestions.

A woman alone at home was menaced by drug dealers who thought she was someone else. Sylvia turned that one off. Israeli spies. No. A child is murdered, and no one in the small town knows who did it, unless they all know and it's only the detective who's in the dark. Sylvia kept that one going for a while. The woman the detective questioned was sleeping with the husband of the woman across the street. Sylvia didn't have one single neighbor worth having an affair with. Once one of them had come over in tight bicycle shorts. She was utterly repelled by the snug black wrapping on his thighs and the bulging genital package overshadowed by an unathletic paunch. The worst of it was that he traipsed around in that gear all the time and surely hadn't meant it as alluring. It was just gross.

People in a town in Alaska are utterly cut off from the outside by a blizzard. Children are being put into a coma by some unknown force. An old, battered policeman who was just passing through and who left the town thirty years earlier begins to suss out something. The old, battered policeman meets the woman he had wanted to marry. She appears at least twenty years younger than him, though they were supposedly high school sweethearts. He's gray and worn, but she hasn't aged, because women shouldn't. She sweeps her blonde hair back behind her ears with dissatisfaction while she ices cupcakes in her café. She's an independent businesswoman. Her husband died in a freak accident several years earlier. Her lips are incredibly shapely. Sylvia almost got up to look at her own lips in the bathroom mirror, but didn't. She was pretty sure she wouldn't like what she saw. The cupcake woman and the detective drew close and almost kissed. A strange light flashed in the sky. They went outside to look at it.

While it's pretty clear that the old, battered detective will eventually face off with the old, wicked predator who has built an underground lab in the remote Alaskan town and is using the town's children as research subjects, three episodes later, not much is resolved. Sylvia missed half of it through nodding off.

"Mom, wake up," Jordan said. He went into the bathroom, cutting her off from it when she really needed to pee. He stayed in there interminably, probably anointing himself with his acne medicine and examining his hair. She almost went and peed in the sink, but when she shouted to him a second time, he came out. He brushed past her without a glance. A sad melody seeped out from under his door when she went by after turning out lights and making sure everything was locked. "Good night, sweetie," she called. If he made a little grunt in acknowledgment, she didn't hear it.

The Flowers of Tarbes

Who am I, the I of this book? She appears here and there, looking out her window, visiting her family, and sitting at her computer producing letters, words, lines, and paragraphs. Does she do it just for fun? I had a chart once where I checked off the days I was able to write, in the early morning before the kids woke up. When I hadn't written, I scribbled my excuses: *Bronchitis. Up all night. Delia sick.* The entire family, all four of us, slept at that point on a mattress on the floor. I left the bedroom on hands and knees, both to not wake them up and because I felt so weak. I crawled down the hall between the bedroom and the corner with my desk and pecked away, without even making coffee. Sometimes I fell asleep by seven at night, while reading to the kids. They lay awake on either side of me, while I found the unconsciousness that was supposed to be theirs. I faded in and out between sentences, returning to read the same words over again, maybe continuing to read while I slept, then waking further down the page, then tumbling off again.

I didn't witness this scene, but I can see it as if from above, the kids with their eyes bright, my daughter holding a handful of my hair, my son idly kicking his feet. I'm the absent one, the blank in the middle. At some point, at four-thirty or five, I got up again. It would have been easier to stay in bed. But I've been chipping away at it. Out of this domesticity, tunneling towards a deeper note. A story I want to tell, about terror.

I made Sylvia and Marina up, or extrapolated their existence. If the transcripts of the detainees at Abu Ghraib were typed, then someone did the typing. If those photos were given captions or numbers, logged as evidence, someone wrote down those phrases or identifying tags.

Nimble fingers had to have operated in this world. These are the people who brought this story to me, and so to you.

There are many other things I could be writing about, for instance polar exploration, or the anguish of a daughter whose mother disappeared in a boating accident. At some point, maybe five or six years ago, I got stuck on the simple eloquence of the detainees' phrases, such as "They took our clothes off, even the underwear, and they beat us very hard." The vocabulary is precise. The actions are clear. The recrimination arises in the fantastic process of not heeding, not responding to these statements. The detainees' words seem to set off a whole collaborative mechanism of undoing, a world in reverse that swallows up and ignores. What a mysterious place, and how orderly and contained it strives to be.

The writer inserted a note of complaint here: while I'm highlighting her persistence, she feels she doesn't get enough credit for her craft. She claims it's very difficult, as she has to not only "pick the exact right word but to shape the narrative so the reader hangs on." She says she's responsible for "sweeping the street as well as conducting a parade over it." She's already been compared to a servant standing at the sideboard. She doesn't want to be mistaken for a domestic drudge.

Well, that's the risk she takes. Without this writer character, we'd never get to those curious asides about the poet Ponge and all the other intrusions that break up the inevitable onflow. She pauses here to tell us a little more about Ponge's friend and mentor, the editor and critic Jean Paulhan. A complicated man, he encouraged Ponge while, as has been noted, not bothering to give any comments on the poet's unsatisfactory first draft of his masterpiece, "Soap."

Paulhan, like Ponge, was in the Resistance. Paulhan was captured and tortured, but he survived. He wrote the foreword to the erotic novel *The Story of O*, a book in letters about a woman enslaving herself to a man who pimps her out. It's said the masterful lover the letters are addressed to was in reality Paulhan. However, he wrote the preface as if he had no connection to the story. He promoted many French

Angela Woodward

writers through the journal he edited, but he remained in the background himself. He wrote a book on terror in literature, called *The Flowers of Tarbes.*

This is the story of the flowers of Tarbes: There's a park in a town called Tarbes. Imagine it's a delightful place full of tulips, lilacs, roses in their seasons. At the entrance to this public park hangs a sign. The sign reads, "It Is Forbidden to Enter the Park Carrying Flowers."

Paulhan has a lot of other things to say about terror in literature. But this little paragraph is all he says about the flowers of Tarbes. So cruel. Don't look to me to explain what he means. I've roped Paulhan in because he's on my side. Stand there, reading this prohibition painted on plywood, carefully bolted to the iron gate. What's happening to you? And what should you do? You never even thought to bring flowers to the park. But now you can't. You're forbidden.

Gus and Jayda

Really just Jayda, but Gus figured in Marina's narratives as a foil. He was a fat, happy four-year-old, a complacent love bug, or so Marina said. She described Jayda's hysterics, followed by a cameo of Gus looking sleepy and bringing his mom his pillow.

"You won't believe what she's scared of now," Marina said, having come in late after a conference at Jayda's school.

Sylvia removed the headphones and looked across the empty middle of the room towards her officemate. Marina stood next to her own desk, combing her hair and applying lipstick while supplying Sylvia with the latest Jayda antics. The little girl had a revulsion for socks, which was okay most of the year in their climate. She hated history in school so much that she had to be excused, and Marina had to read and quiz her on the Founding Fathers on her own time. It was something to do with the lack of bathrooms and heat back then that made Jayda so upset she couldn't sit still. Her latest was a fear of the color green, for a reason Jayda wouldn't divulge.

"They blame me for it, of course," Marina said, clicking open her little compact mirror and checking her lips again.

"There's a lot of green things to avoid," Sylvia said.

"Salad, broccoli, books with green covers, fields." Marina speculated it had to do with Jayda's friend Allie reading horse books, and Jayda liking Babysitter's Club. It might have had to do with an illustration in Allie's pony book, or a dream Jayda had about the pony book, or about stepping on something at the fake grass soccer gym her dad took her to. "Bruce has no clue," she said, meaning her ex-husband. Marina got on great with her ex. They were best friends, and would still be married if it wasn't for Bruce's drinking, gambling, and poverty. They had talked for hours about Jayda's weird anxieties, and he had shown up for the meeting with the teacher. Even so, Jayda's phobias were Marina's fault. "Guilty, guilty, guilty!" she said. She moved around her desk and looked at the wires connecting the Dictaphone. She stretched her arms over her head. "What a mess," she said.

"Jordan's teachers all give me the most pitiful looks," Sylvia contributed. "I think it's because I came to teacher's night in sweats, that time the washer broke." Parents at her son's school dressed exquisitely. She had realized too late that it was a competition.

"They think I'm a freak. What can I do? I said, 'She's always been like this,' and Mrs. Markson nods her head, like, 'Obviously.'" Marina sat herself down and disappeared into the headphones.

"They took our clothes off, even the underwear, and they beat us very hard," Sylvia typed. "When I told them I am sick, they laughed at me and beat me." She looked up and found Marina looking at her.

"Doesn't her name sort of mean green?" Sylvia asked. She repeated the question while Marina freed her ears.

"It's J-A-Y-da. Not J-A-D-E."

"I know. But didn't you get her those jade earrings?"

Jayda, whom Sylvia had never met, seemed to be the ultimate girly beauty, had had her ears pierced when she was a toddler, wore her ballet tutu to kindergarten. Marina sometimes apologized for telling Sylvia about Jayda's cute shoes or sparkly nails, the only times her office mate really pissed Sylvia off. Marina implied Sylvia felt a lack, from not having a daughter. She didn't.

"Oh god. I hope she forgot all that." Sylvia clearly remembered Marina feeding her daughter some myth about the green stone because Jayda didn't like her actual birthstone. Sylvia didn't know what her own birthstone was. "It's nothing," Marina said. "Who knows. I just hope it doesn't last."

The two women went back to their machines.

Urine II

The immature are known for having no coordination of their urine. They need to be cleaned. Baby possums are the exception and possibly take care of that themselves. The act of a horse urinating can be described as "staling," a more polite and distinct word for the livestock's exudation. Those involved with horses day to day probably say "pissing" like the rest of us. It's usually a dire circumstance when piss or pee gets designated "urine." The urinator is in the realm of someone else's control: Has he urinated? Has he passed urine?

When a body gets into the situation where its elimination system is described scientifically or formally, that body is in trouble, as in "They took me to a closed room and poured water on me, and forced me to put my head in someone's urine that was already in that room." Here we can wonder whether the translator did a little more than put these statements into English. Two translators actually signed off on each document. The one may have said, "Let's say 'urine' here," not pussyfooting around with the head and the floor, but substituting the more scientific and medical term for the vulgar "piss."

The body needs to cleanse itself from the inside, thus its clever system of passing water imbued with waste products out of the body through a series of tubes and a small hole. Only mothers, in most cases, can squirt another liquid, the milk made in their breasts, through an array of pores around the nipples. Women without children might never experience this, and men are left out of the game altogether, except for that other product, semen. The infant sucks the milk from the mother's breast, the second breast leaking all over the place. Later, the infant pees, without even knowing she's doing it. It just comes out. No tension, no effort, no expectation.

Urine can be dried, and its chemical or alchemical elements abstracted, but it's in general not dark enough to be used as ink. It can be drunk, in dire circumstances, or in the case of a particular pleasure, not shared by all, of having a woman squat over one's mouth and pee into it. Urine can keep the stranded traveler alive for many days, if the traveler can figure out how to capture their own pee in a tarp or cup. It can be sucked out of cloth, but in that process a lot of the liquid is wasted. If a traveler can convince an animal, say a turtle, to urinate in a convenient place, then the traveler may stay alive a few more days. Maybe the traveler graduates from the turtle to a lizard to drinking the urine of a beautiful fox. The traveler, when presented at last with a plant stem filled with a sweet, life-sustaining sap, might still feel a bit cheated that an animal even larger and more beautiful than the fox didn't stop for him. Plants do not urinate.

The urine of pregnant mares is captured and strained for its beneficent hormones. Mare's urine becomes a smooth white estrogen cream when mixed with ingredients like wax, glycerin, and cetyl alcohol. Though it's not advisable to pee directly onto plants, diluted urine applied to the soil is an excellent fertilizer. The earth itself, groaning and heaving through space, adorns itself with forests and fields mainly because of the kind action of the urine of animals on its rocky surface. "They took me to a closed room and poured water on me, and forced me to put my head in someone's urine that was already in that room," one of the detainees told his interviewer. "After that they beat me with a broom and stepped on my head while it was still in the urine."

"Let's not say 'piss' here," one of the translators might have said. "Change that to 'urine.'" Perhaps this makes it gentler on the reader, who's now been deferred to as a scientific, judicial type. This reader will be spared street slang and profanity. Or "urine" was the gift of the translator to the man whose head was in it. The word accords the beaten man some solemnity. Now he's the judicial one, corralling his experiences into this rigid vocabulary. "Urine" gives his statement more heft. It's impossible to pinpoint who this word "urine" was meant to honor. Two translators signed off on the statement's accuracy. They must have had to come to an agreement with each other. They must have sorted through alternative phrasings, and maybe asked for advice. Their names are on the documents too, along with the name of their employer: Titan Corporation Inc.

Sylvia transcribed the session, putting in proper margins, paragraphs, and punctuation. Her actions made the whole thing readable. Legible. There wouldn't be a story at all without these typists getting all the details right. "They opened the water in the cell and told us to lay face down in the water. We stayed like that until the morning, naked, without clothes."

After an hour, Sylvia got up and walked down the hall to the Ladies. She sat on the cold white bowl, latched behind a solid plate of gray faux marble. Sylvia peed into the clean toilet almost without noticing the hot splash and pleasure of release. It was the most human thing she'd done all day. She pulled up her undies and her uncomfortable nylons, and smoothed everything down under her skirt. All dressed up, Sylvia could have passed for an animal without any openings at all.

She rinsed her hands off with just water. The whole Ladies stank of pee, disinfectant, and the horrible new soap. Even though she had complained to Alex and brought her own soap, nothing had changed. It smelled abominable in there. No one had done anything about it.

Urine III

Marina didn't make it in until almost ten. Then Audrey came in to tell her she had a call from the school. "Don't they have my cell?" she asked Audrey, but Audrey wouldn't know anything about that.

Marina came back from Audrey and Georgia's office, mouthed goodbye to Sylvia, and sped away.

"Is everything okay?" Sylvia asked when Marina returned just before noon, bearing a styrofoam platter of fries and a shake.

Marina slurped through her straw emphatically. This served as an answer for a while. Sylvia folded up her sandwich crumbs in her napkin and tucked it into the trash. The peel of the banana she'd eaten earlier stared up at her, along with a collection of caramel wrappers. She hardly remembered eating the caramels, but the evidence was there. "I'm taking a turn," Sylvia said. This was their term for a little break spent roaming the hallway, just to get out of the room. Sylvia went out the side door that didn't have a security guard and stood in the tiny concrete picnic area. A man and woman sat on the smoker's bench, smoking. She went back in through the front door, showing her badge to the guy at the desk. She sat down and put on the headphones. "After that they beat me with a broom and stepped on my head while it was still in the urine," she typed. Marina's head was bent over the typewriter, fingers in motion.

Sylvia took some time to think about calling Jordan's choir teacher about the costume. "I'm going to make a call," she told Marina. Marina didn't look up. That was reason enough for Sylvia not to make the call. It could wait one more day.

"I don't know what I'll find when I get to that school," Marina said at the end of the day.

"Good luck," Sylvia said. She took it that Marina didn't want her to pry. The next day she got the whole story, that Jayda had peed in her pants and had to be cleaned up in the nurse's office and given a pair of track pants kept in a laundry basket under the nurse's desk. Jayda refused to wear the too-big track pants, so Marina had to go get her, take her home, give her a bath, and find her something else to wear, while Jayda cried and complained the whole time.

"Poor kid," Sylvia said. "What's going on?"

"Who knows. If I have to do that all over again today, I'll hang myself."

It was just an expression.

Show Choir Costume II

"What I was wondering, Ms. Wells," Sylvia began after all the pleasantries were over, "is whether we could rent the costume for the concert instead of buying it. He's still growing, you know, he loves the choir, I'm sure he'll want to do it next year, and the pants, if they're too short on him next year, I wouldn't want to waste the money."

Ms. Wells, who had been chatty and effusive, switched over to a tone she must have learned from the dean of her education program when she got her master's. Sylvia recognized the vocabulary and politeness of talking to a "family in need," and it was as if she were conversing with an ambassador rather than Jordan's show choir director. Sylvia listened politely, saying "uh huh, uh huh" when necessary, as Ms. Wells went through the contract with the tailoring company, the school's financial literacy program, and how the school encouraged entrepreneurship and self-determination.

"But if I rent something just like it, is that okay?" Sylvia broke in. "We could just buy the vest."

Ms. Wells repeated all the rigmarole about financial literacy over again, and added more about the history of jazz. Sylvia couldn't figure out how that related. The kids loved Ms. Wells because she was young. It was horrible being older than her kid's teachers. The elementary school teachers had all been in their forties and fifties, and Sylvia herself had been younger back then.

At last she got clearance to rent the pants and suit jacket. The red sequined vest was a special item that had to be bought from the equipment company the school contracted with. Ms. Wells said she would ask a recent grad if he would loan his out. "And the tie, of course," she said, as if that was an extra bonus she was offering completely free, but that she might withhold if Sylvia wasn't grateful enough.

"We'd love to have the loan of those items," Sylvia said, becoming an honorary consul herself. Sylvia didn't know why this conversation was so difficult. As if no one had ever wanted to get out of buying the expensive costume before. It was probably because Ms. Wells hadn't been at the school very long.

Ink

It's difficult to find a precise formula for modern ink. The documents that Sylvia and Marina typed concerning the torture and injury of countless detained men are sitting right there on the Internet for anyone to learn about, but ink makers keep the exact ingredients of their product secret. Though chemists can take ink apart and identify its components, the proportions and processes are proprietary and can't be disclosed. Don't bother asking. The historians of ink in the last century had as much trouble with this as I had. The secret of a truly black ink disappeared in Europe after the fall of Rome. Many documents faded to gray or brown. It mattered less, as fewer people were literate. Even kings could do no more than draw an X for their name. It's a wonder that our civilization even kept trying with ink. Those wanting their words to carry on into the future found other means. They scratched letters into animal bones. Inscriptions on bells and signs woven into tapestries rivaled books. Market vendors and gamblers conducted business with a look, a handshake, a nod, or just the silence of implied agreement.

So-called fugitive inks wasted in daylight. An embezzler or careless assistant could easily obliterate a signed contract with a wet sponge. To punish a wicked woman, a priest wrote curses on paper and then washed the maledictions into water. He obliged the offender to drink it. In this case, ink's malleability was useful. Ink made with galls came out muddy and deteriorated quickly. An ink made with yeast, cuttlefish ink, and pomegranate rind wrote fine dark letters at first use, but never lasted.

Fortunately, ink wasn't only for writing. Doctors applied a paste of slightly reduced ink made from blue copperas, ox glue, and the smoke from torches to gangrenous flesh. An injured leg might turn blue, purple, green, and then black, protesting its decay in these signals on the skin. The black gunk smeared on it might speak to the force beneath that was composing the limb's demise. Healers snipped holy letters out of ancient documents, ground them into a paste with almonds and other ingredients, and sold the ointment to those seeking health or luck, or the opposite. Scavengers hauled old scrolls out of libraries and sold them for heating fuel. The ink made from smoke returned to smoke.

The various men who invented the typewriter fretted over its inked ribbon. Too wet and the ink splashed coronas around the edges of the letters; too dry and the impression wasn't readable. They also had to get the elasticity of the fabric right, and create a mechanism that turned the ribbon on a spindle so that a fresh mark could be made. Early typists mailed away their used ribbons to have them reinked by the typewriter manufacturer. Some of the typists inserted a brief note into the used ribbon package, exclaiming about how much more they could accomplish on the new machine versus their old days of writing by hand. In either case, they came home with their fingerprints picked out in gray and with smudges under their eyes and on their sleeves.

Sylvia and Marina spent all day at their machines, except for those breaks of using the Ladies, walking the corridors of the office building, eating lunch in the break room or at their desks, making phone calls, or sitting staring at nothing. Despite all this, their hands didn't show it. Sylvia couldn't be bothered to care for her nails, while Marina painted hers red, white, yellow, gold, whatever she wanted. Sylvia's fingertips got an icky feeling that translated up her arms from the slight greasiness of the carbonless forms. She didn't know if Marina felt the same. The smell in the room struck her hard when she opened the door in the morning. The oil from the typewriters, the dust accumulating on the electrical cords, the stale food, and the scent of the women's shampoos and lotions collaborated into a particular concoction. The smell that was so strong at nine a.m. was even more noticeable by ten. She really couldn't stand it. Someone had to do something about it.

Ink

A PDF of a document sometimes looks on-screen like a faded type-written piece, with little abrasions in the corners of letters so that *and* looks like *ard.* The whole thing can appear worn and washed out, unlike a document freshly composed and still in process. This is usually only when the reader has clicked on the document to open it but hasn't downloaded it yet. The downloaded version is in my experience always clearer.

The PDF was invented in the early nineties. It was a valuable solution to the inability of documents made by many different word processing programs to pass from computer to computer unchanged, and to print out successfully on a variety of machines. The PDF's inventor was concerned mostly with documents for businesses, but also speculated about the transmission of magazine articles, value-line stock charts, Time Life books, and military maps.

For some reason, I sometimes can't get PDFs to print out. I'm not the only one. I remember a friend telling me he had to use his work printer to print out a PDF I'd sent him. He couldn't get his home printer to do it. He probably hadn't updated some software he should have updated. He probably felt at fault, and maybe wondered why he wanted the pages in his hands instead of sitting and reading on-screen.

I've had vicious arguments with people about e-readers versus printed books. I never understood why they wanted to defend their technology so hard, but these conversations always grew heated. I'm really in favor of both, but I would somehow get cast as the poor technophobe. Someone who I was at least sort of friends with reviled me for taking big, fat *Anna Karenina* on a trip instead of loading up my e-reader with a dozen e-books. So ridiculous. I have no idea why so much was at stake, but that was basically our last conversation. Reading is so wonderful, turning the pages of a book, the smell of the paper, the quiet rustle of the page falling onto its fellows, the little panic when you've turned two pages at once and find yourself faced with a gap in your understanding. Touching the bottom of the screen of the lit-up reader is also magical, the kind and unnoticeable refabrication of the next and necessary page right at the instant you desire it.

The invention of the PDF involves terms such as raster, stretching, and cache. You'd almost think they were talking about rare earths or warbler toes, the vocabulary becomes so arcane. The inventor of the PDF felt very bad about two-pixel- versus three-pixel-width pieces of font, and how dreadful they looked when their differences weren't accounted for. I've seen quite a lot of vociferousness in considerations of ink formulas. The same high emotions govern discussion of the representation of fonts on-screen. I can hardly intervene, but it seems to me the PDF solved some problems we didn't know we had. We should be grateful.

I used to read library books in the bathtub, with a towel draped over the rim of the tub. I carefully wiped my fingers dry before turning the page. I never once dropped a whole book into the water. Librarians don't approve of this practice and warn against it. I haven't obeyed them so much as given up the exercise. These days when I take a bath, I stare at the taps and the tile. I enjoy the steam and the warmth, but I can't bring myself to read at all. I couldn't say why. I just can't read much anymore.

Ice III

I went out on the frozen lake behind my house at last. I'd been taking walks up on the bluffs by the effigy mound park a few days in a row. I saw a family out on the ice, mother, father, little girl, and dog. On the bench behind what would be the beach of the park in summertime, an elderly couple sat, lacing snowshoes onto their boots. These seemed to be the kind of people who knew the ice was safe. I changed my tack and stepped sideways down the steep track.

The dog bounded up to me, but after that I didn't speak to anyone. Snow fell heavily, and I could barely make out the buildings on the other side of the lake. They stood there bleached out, a building-like haze. In the middle, almost nothing, just white on white. Snow on top of ice, and snow filling the air. Way in the distance, a tiny figure moved away from me on skis. The figure had an exaggerated, perfect left-right movement, like an illustration or a cartoon of a skier. At one point I thought the figure was skiing backwards. Then I understood that without my noticing, the figure had turned and was now skiing towards me extremely slowly. The wind came right under my hat, and I hadn't brought my second pair of gloves.

I've been out there in other years in the moonlight. I went once with someone very dear to me then. Only when we came back onto land and then into my warm house did I realize that we hadn't spoken the whole time. It was the fullest point of our intimacy, that it was wordless.

The sight that's almost an absence of sight, the total whiteness except for the far horizon, is one part of the experience of walking on the ice. As strong is the sound of flakes from the sky cutting into the flakes already fallen. The crunch of boots. And nothing else.

Soap IV

"I'm going to go find Alex," Sylvia said, though Marina didn't look up. "This whole place smells so terrible."

Sylvia thought she felt the flick of Marina's gaze as she went out the door. She hesitated, then felt bad about moving on down the hall. Something was really bothering Marina. She was jumpy and forgetful. She had made some mistakes on her forms that she showed to Sylvia, getting the numbers wrong for a whole series, all off by three digits, the one error compounding into all the ones that came after it. Sylvia told her she had to go back and redo them. Alex had already taken the folders. It didn't seem to Sylvia and Marina that anyone checked up on them. Their errors so far hadn't been flung in their faces. But still. When it was this obvious that Marina had screwed up, she had better go back and do those forms over. Marina said she would, but Sylvia wasn't sure that she had. She wasn't in charge of Marina.

Sylvia's errand concerned the soap in the Ladies again. She knocked on the partition that was Alex's cubicle. Though for a while the bathrooms on the third floor still used the old soap, now there was no place left to go. The new, putrid pink filled the dispensers everywhere, and her only recourse would have been to leave the building to wash her hands.

"I put in a request for you," Alex said, blinking. He looked so young, but he was probably one of those young-looking men who really wasn't. "Even though you're the only one who's complained."

"And Marina. There's two of us."

"I did what I could. I don't have control over everything that goes on here. It's probably not that high a priority."

"It's making me sick!"

Alex refrained from answering, letting his slightly curved lips transform the longer she looked, from a soft agreeing smile to a derisive disdain of her pettiness, without a muscle moving.

"If I'm allergic to it . . ."

"I don't want you to suffer," he said.

Sylvia underwent one of her few sweeps of rage. Tears came to her eyes, and she felt a flood of color and heat wash upwards from her navel, probably making her look vulnerable and ridiculous. She could hear him thinking that it must be her time of the month or some other female fallibility that made her care so much about something so trivial.

"What about that sick building report?" Even as she said it, she remembered that of course it wasn't this building that had had a possible and ultimately unproven case of formaldehyde in the HVAC. It was the old building down the block, where they used to work. It was very much like this one, once you got inside. Alex was able to keep his lip crescent going. It now registered laughter at her expense as he confirmed how ignorant and emotional she was. The more Sylvia recorded his reaction to her as arrogant, the less she could think of anything that might help her case. Her throat was so tight she couldn't even speak. Telling him what a vile little prick he was would turn him against her. Yet it seemed so true.

"This is all I'm asking," she said, with a big gravelly stumble in the middle of it. "I haven't asked for anything else."

Alex changed his smile into a broader one and nodded his head to go with it. "The new soap," he said, "is antimicrobial."

Sylvia struggled for a response, but "antimicrobial" hung between the two of them, lending its prestige to Alex's team.

Alex watched her take the hit, then swiveled his torso back to his computer screen. From where Sylvia stood, she couldn't see what was on it. Probably an order for Post-it notes to their employer's contracted office supply supplier.

When she got back to the room, Marina was on her cell. The signal inside was terrible, and they usually didn't even try. They went to the spot in the hall that got a stronger signal, or went outside. "I'm sorry too," Marina was saying. "Yes, yes, I know."

She hung up right away, but it was more the tone Sylvia caught, a smooth, satiny underpinning. Mr. Right, whatever his name was, was still in the picture. Marina smiled down at her lap, then cast a wide, open joyfulness Sylvia's way.

Ink

Some inks of the past cut fine, dark lines into paper and then continued to cut. A pile of documents, say a will, or the deed to some land and warehouses, might sit in a lawyer's credenza for years. When the heirs or the business partners came to look over these records, they found the ink had bitten right through the paper. Its acidity ground up the cotton rag, and the writing of the grandfather's or businessman's lawyer had transformed into a series of tiny, letter-shaped windows. The heirs still might have been able to read the documents, but only slowly, straining their eyes to make out the words as shadows on a wall in angled light.

Certain inks made with wood galls dribbled out of the pen nib a purplish gray. These inks darkened as they oxidized, so that whatever had been written in them seemed louder, surer, and more emphatic the more time passed. Magicians, peddlers, or even nannies and elder sisters made tricks with special inks. They drew a winter scene in stout black lines and then drew over it springtime flowers and birds in trees with colored inks. These colors faded away instantly, but they roused again when warmed. A kind nanny asked a little girl to hold the drawing of a dreary winter woodland up to the fire. The girl cried out as the grass seemed to grow and daisies sprouted between the trunks. By bedtime, the yellow birds and blue toadstools had faded away. This miracle could be repeated many times until the little girl's carelessness took the whole thing away in flames.

The squid blots itself out with its own ink as it flees, creating a cloud of black where once there was an animal. Its ink is called sepia and isn't much good on its own. Once in New York I watched an auction for crates of letters rescued from a sunken liner. Their addresses still clung bravely to the greened and spotted envelopes. The collectors sat still on wooden chairs, competing avidly with tiny gestures. They wanted the mark the post office had inked across the envelopes, *LOST AT SEA*. This brilliant red had lost none of its color.

> Stark's ink, Runge's chrome ink, alizarine ink
> (which contains Dutch madder and Aleppo galls),
> invisible ink, ink that poisons the reading eye
> or taints the finger that turns the page
> mixed with glue from stag, cattle, or fish
> likewise soot, varnish, egg white

An electrician created a magic screen, where aluminum powder and plastic beads conspired to draw inkless lines at the turn of a knob. With a shake, the lines disappeared. The Etch A Sketch was not ink but the absence of ink, and yet this might be the important factor. Ink pretends to keep on, to penetrate, to make dark, to confirm suspicions. People will do anything to acquire this sense of permanence.

A writer of my avidity, if she was born, say, in the eighteenth century, would have made her own ink, fermenting it carefully in a warm spot by the hearth for a good two weeks before it could be used. If she hadn't planned ahead enough to carry out this domestic task, the writer may have dipped into the bluing kept in the laundry. This concoction kept clean sheets from looking yellow, and it could be used in an emergency to write pale pastel imprecations. If the writer had more money than time, she might have run out into the street when she heard the cry of the ink seller. This roaming ink man might have stopped his donkey and siphoned a bit of ink out of a barrel into the writer's little ink pot. Doubtless his hands were filthy, and the combination of the donkey's aroma with the acrid perfume of the ink set a scene for all the senses.

The writer of course may have had no access to this substance because of lack of time, money, ingredients, or the freedom to interact with commercial travelers or stationers. She may have been making ink, and wine, and pickled onions, for others, and scarcely written a word herself. The writer may have written words in snow or in dirt with a stick. She may have taken a path through the woods, and seen a huge old elm tree toppled over. Where a flap of bark had come undone, she saw the scribblings of beetles, their chew marks incised as dark lines on the pale wood. The lines curved and crossed, the collective work of anonymous authors. The beetles insist on making marks, and we could even say the insects make meaning, if we count the wonder and consternation of the witness. These cryptic and illegible strokes called out to the writer: Anyone can do it! All it takes is some determination!

I'm spending my time writing about writings that are clear and easy to read, that sit there on the Internet, indexed by search engines, entered into public and legal records. The story begins, "They took me into a room and beat me. On another occasion I was forced to lie down while MPs jumped onto my back and legs." Yet it may be that the secret mouth marks of the beetles, disclosed only after considerable decay of the tree trunk, call up more profound feelings in their readers. The insects move us to openness, to wonder what it all means. The documents I've persisted in dragging in front of you call up unease and shame. They're so clear. They're so direct. They're neatly typed, signed and dated.

We might give some thought to that stiff phrase "On another occasion." It's as if there had been a series of meetings logged into a calendar, rather than days and nights smeared into one long nightmare. Someone who saw himself as merely transmitting the language of one person into the language of another in order to create a record of the events must have suggested this particular expression. There's at least a sliver of uncertainty. Someone at some point had intervened. "And then," or "later," or "another time" may have sounded too casual to the translator. There's more of the implied rebuke in the formal rendering, "On another occasion." A retention of dignity for the speaker.

I imagine a small scene, maybe entirely silent, of an employee of Titan Corporation Inc. hunched over a notebook, a desk lamp shining

Angela Woodward

a pool of yellow onto a cluttered table. Here this person sits, tapping a ballpoint against his teeth. He writes in a lined notebook. He crosses something out. He sighs. He writes something else in over his scribble. It takes a long time to weigh and settle on the exact right word.

Flowers

Audrey came in with a big bouquet of daisies. Sylvia didn't look up until Audrey was right in front of her. The slightly antiseptic smell caused her to raise her head, and the flowers loomed, tilted towards her. It was like a fairy godmother had appeared in the typists' room, because Sylvia had missed the door opening and closing and the sound of footsteps. Audrey might have descended from the ceiling or appeared out of a cloud of glitter. Sylvia pushed the headphones down around her neck in time to say, "Watch out!" Audrey was about to spill water out of the vase. Sylvia shouted this super loud, not adjusting to being able to hear her own voice like a normal person. "Sorry, sorry," she said. "What've you got?"

"They're for Marina, but you girls can't take deliveries here. You know that."

Sylvia actually didn't know that. It hadn't been stressed, though it might have been noted somewhere in the staff manual. She wondered if that was why Alex was always bugging them about pad thai. He was supposed to handle lunch orders for all of them.

Audrey fussed around for a place to put the vase down. She took up a handful of the finished transcript forms and shook them together into a neat pile. Sylvia held back a scream. At her audible intake of air, Audrey looked up. Her eyes flicked down to the pages, then back to Sylvia's face, which must have been a mug of round eyes with black circles under them, plucked eyebrows arched high, and a mouth held half open by tight cheeks. Audrey set the pages down.

"We're supposed to put them in the folders, and Alex takes them. Sorry, Audrey."

"Sorry," Audrey said.

Both the women breathed carefully, making happen something that could have happened automatically and without any conscious intention. Sylvia had taken her foot off the Dictaphone pedal, but the hissing still poured out of the open headphone cups under her chin. It was like one long snoring inhale, with an exhale that never arrived. Audrey's eyes, cast down, took in the desk surface next to Sylvia, the open bottle of correction fluid with its sticky brush lying in a pool of its own liquid, a curled bag of chips and two coffee cups, and the detritus of triplicate pages Sylvia had not attempted to neaten up. Sylvia felt scalded by Audrey's glance. Her desk had seemed just fine until the other woman looked at it.

Audrey met Sylvia's eyes with a brisk cheerfulness bandaged over the face of a moment ago. "Won't Marina be surprised," she said.

Sylvia took the headphones all the way off, and the two women crossed the room together. Sylvia made space on Marina's desk and Audrey set the vase down. Gus as a baby, Jayda in a ballet costume, Gus in Jayda's lap, Gus and Jayda both leaning their heads into a smiling Marina's neck, and a distant shot of the three of them against a signpost for a state park witnessed the placement of the flowers from Marina's bulletin board. A few seconds later Marina herself appeared, back from the Ladies probably.

"Oh my god!" she said. "What's the occasion?"

"You should know," Sylvia said, while Audrey explained in really the nicest way possible that "you girls" weren't allowed to accept deliveries of packages or food or flowers or anything at work. Marina should have asked her beau to send the flowers to her home.

"I'm sorry," Marina said. "I didn't know anything about it. I don't even know how he has this address."

"They're lovely," Audrey said.

The three of them stared at the spectacle crowning Marina's desk, the clean white petals springing off the yellow centers and the surrounding mist of baby's breath and fern. Marina opened the card, looked it over, and folded it back into its little envelope without saying anything. Sylvia assumed the flowers were a statement from Mr. Right, but she refrained from any comment. They must have made up their differences. If he wasn't married already, maybe he wanted to marry her, or just say he was sorry for whatever dickish way he had treated her.

Audrey seemed to be trying to radiate good cheer and approval in order to counteract her scolding. She cleared her throat, but didn't speak, moving her mouth back to her slight smile. Her fingertips rested lightly on the desk, making a stripe of blouse cuff fall out from under her blazer sleeve. The daisies radiated a light chemical odor, and the white of the petals gleamed under the haze of the overhead fixtures. All three women stood stiffly, unable to get themselves out of the tableau the flowers had arranged them into.

Car Wash

Jordan's show choir was holding a car wash to raise money for their trip to Florida. Sylvia had had to get up at six to drive Jordan to school. Neither of them had spoken the entire trip. She went back to bed, then roused herself to go out and do some errands. On the way back, she swung by the school parking lot for the car wash. She had promised.

A bevy of young faces smiled at her from the curb. She noticed their straight teeth, boys and girls alike outfitted with white chompers like actors or models. Jordan's friend Parrish's older sister Emma was in show choir. "Hi, Sylvia!" she called out, waving her giant sponge.

Emma leaned in the window, her hair escaping her hoodie and beating against the frame of the car. She promised a super wash, super clean, and it was for a good cause. "I did this last year for Forensics, too," she said. "This is way more personal than a regular car wash."

"Jordan made me come," she said.

Emma laughed. They were totally on par, the young woman with straight teeth and a full life of college, music, and adventure in front of her, and her little brother's friend's mother, who was on the downhill slope of all that. Sylvia grasped for an advantage over this healthy creature. She should at least appear wise, or in control of her own finances and destiny. But really it wasn't that way, and Emma's offer of equality was condescending.

Three more of Jordan's show choir gang came up with their sponges and began swiping up and down. A tall redhead leaned over the windshield, authoritatively plucking up the wipers so they didn't get in the way of her squeegee. Sylvia rolled up the window, cutting off the music the kids had on behind them on a boom box. The energized but mournful tune was loud enough that it still scraped through. Two of them who weren't occupied with cars sang along. The wind whipped their hair horizontal. It had to be really chilly to have wet hands and no shelter in the parking lot.

At last she figured out where Jordan was. He stepped away from the other car they'd been working on, two bills hanging out of his hand. He held the money up triumphantly, walking over to the girl who held the cash box. She and the girls by the boom box screamed. They all high-fived.

The wipers clunked back into place, and the kids buffing Sylvia's car descended. They must have been cleaning the hubcaps.

Jordan knocked on the window. "Hi, Mom," he said, smiling.

"I said I'd come. Aren't you cold?"

"No!" His face tightened. She was always criticizing him, he implied.

"Good job, Jordie, getting your mom out," Emma said. The other kids gawked, their sponges and implements dripping. Sylvia compared her car to the one Jordan had just finished cleaning. The school was plump with that kind of buxom suburban van. Her little thirteen-year-old sedan must count as an oddity, if not street cred for Jordan. Plus hers really needed washing. The van had probably come in sparkling already.

The girl with the squeegee got back to work, exaggerating her industry in a cheerful, mocking way, her elbows out, throwing herself into it. Emma ordered the others to go to the curb and relieve the ones who were standing there with their big cardboard signs, waving at traffic. You could have put Emma in charge of a Starbucks, clearly.

"What should I do?" Jordan asked her. Emma sent him over to the boom box. Sylvia watched him walk away, like any other kid. That is, he didn't seem like her kid at the moment, layered in with how he used to be and how she thought of him. His wrists stuck out of his sweatshirt. A long thread frayed off one cuff. This was where he sucked it. He ruined all his sleeves that way.

Sylvia gave Emma a twenty. She whirled away with it, then twisted back towards the car. "Did you want change?"

"I thought it was fifteen?"

Emma smiled brilliantly and ran off. Her ankles flashed over supremely white sneakers. She wasn't wearing socks. She came back with a five and gave it to Sylvia with a warm thanks for coming out this morning. It was too late to give the five back. Emma wouldn't take it. "No, no, of course not," she said, smiling even more sunnily. Sylvia poked the bill out the window and threatened to let the wind take it, but Emma still said no.

It was a pay-what-you-can car wash, fifteen suggested. It seemed like most people paid more. Even by paying the advertised price, Sylvia was revealing herself as stingy or poor.

Sylvia crumpled the five into the cup holder and drove off. Jordan waved, moving his hand stiffly from the wrist, the minimal arc of movement required to register the gesture.

Blood II

Blood can be removed from clothing in a couple ways. First the stain should be soaked in cold water. Hot water makes the blood bond with the fabric, and then it will never come out. Bleach too doesn't do the trick, so anyone relying on their usual practices will get it all backwards and make things worse. Dried blood on a shirt or sweater should be sprayed with an enzymatic cleaner. The kind of person who frequently bleeds all over her sheets or mattress or underwear or who cuts her fingers while chopping parsley or drying wine glasses should go to Walgreens or some other chain drugstore and invest in a special brand of enzymatic cleaner. But most people won't have thought far enough ahead to make this purchase. Most of us will be left with our wits, and regular soap, when it comes to bloodstains. Blood is pernicious in this way, a quality it shares with ink. It's hard to get rid of.

Bloodhounds, and other dogs who are trained to be sensitive, can find one drop of blood in a whole forest. A dog working with the police found a man's murdered wife buried four feet beneath his new concrete patio. A Canadian dog stood on the bow of a boat and directed divers to a man who had drowned in Lake Ontario. In the gray expanse of water and fog, the dog pointed the way, though it wasn't blood alone the cadaver dog sniffed, but putrescence of all sorts. Trainers of these dogs may use their own blood on socks and tennis balls, because a pup trained on rabbit blood may think the game is to find rabbit corpses. Hospitals are sources of waste blood, such as from placentas or surgical rags, but dog trainers would need a confidential relationship with someone in the hospital to get at this stuff. Imagine a hospital administrator looking over a typed request for excess blood from some guy who lives out in the country with a bunch of animals. It's easier for everyone if the trainers use their own blood. It's not that hard to access.

Murderers have been known to write on the wall with their victim's blood. They want to leave a clue, or boast their ideology. People who have been stabbed or shot to death but who take a long time to pass the threshold may also write in their own blood. The victim traces the killer's name on the floor with the blood trickling out of his mouth. In either case, murderer or murdered, the corpse or the crime is not enough of a statement. Words have to be brought into it, with whatever writing fluid is nearest.

Christians can swear oaths with blood, and pass the blood of one congregant to another in a ceremony the priest oversees. The words whispered in the ceremony take on higher qualities when accompanied by blood. "When they took me out of the car, a soldier hit me on the face. Then they stripped me naked and made me crawl the hallway until I was bleeding from my chest to my knees," Sylvia had typed some time ago. In fact months had passed, and it was getting close to the night of Jordan's spring show choir concert.

An account that lacks detail or passion, that is told in a straight-forward way without suspense, is called "bloodless." A man may have bloodless lips, while a woman can paint hers with lipstick with a name like Lady Danger or Enchantress. An account that is full of blood, such as "They stripped me naked and made me crawl the hallway until I was bleeding from my chest to my knees," may still be called "bloodless" if the recitation is carefully modulated to come out as just fact, a series of events. The accounts have been catalogued in documents that might have been lists of serial numbers of tires or geologic features of newly purchased acreage, though the very precision of the details of the body assaulted should make blood flush to the cheeks of the reader.

Blood circulates inside the body, always in transit, and when released from the body, flows towards the lowest point. So too a narrative is in motion, heading towards something. In this case, though I've told you a lot about ink and the poet Ponge, and stopped for a rest with those scenes from Netflix, the two typists of these documents carry the story line forward. Be sure that Mr. Right is doing wrong, and Marina will be forced to face up to it. Sylvia's perception of her son will alter at his show choir concert, which will be a mixture of beauty and sadness. That's where I'm taking you, in hopes that you'll be changed by it.

Blood courses towards the heart, pumping in, pumping out, and going on its way to the far corners of the body. Someone assuredly cleaned up that hallway covered with the detainee's blood, maybe simply by hosing it down. All my trouble to find out about cold versus hot water and enzymatic cleaners is probably beside the point. Dumping a bunch of buckets of any-temperature water would have been sufficient in that case, and even so, no one seemed too worried about the stains there.

Blood has veered us close to a place we've never been, peopling a hallway in a distant prison with men and women assigned to scrub it. Did they have mops? Did they have those wheeled bins that are bucket and conveyance in one, the Royce Rolls? Branching off this hallway, we've at least created the conditions for another room to rise up—one with a desk against a wall, where a translator crosses out "and then" and tries out "on another occasion." Certainly there was a moment of struggle there, to go for the more fluid and idiomatic, or for the stiffly impersonal. Someone has deliberated. Someone has made a choice.

Urine IV

Marina was much more complacent about their work conditions than Sylvia was. Marina sat staring ahead, the headphones around her neck, her mouth open. A series of expressions crossed her face, as if she were in conversation with someone or with herself. Sylvia thought of angling her desk so that she could look up without staring straight at her colleague. She had actually tried moving the thing one morning when Marina was late, but gave up quickly. She could hardly lift one corner of it. Marina hadn't said anything when Sylvia remarked about the strange smell in the room.

"I'm always so negative, aren't I?" Sylvia followed up.

"What?" Marina beamed, crossing out the vaguely curious or anxious expression that had been the last trace of her interior dialog.

"Don't you smell it?"

"It smells like pee in here," Marina said.

"We agree, then."

They both got up and walked around the room. They stood in the doorway looking out. The hall ran away towards the vestibule with the elevator, caught in its weird afternoon light, though it was morning. Marina and Sylvia walked down the hall together and pulled at the door of the janitor's closet. It was locked. Marina thought someone had peed in the hallway. It smelled like a subway, she said. Sylvia hadn't ever been in a subway. They each took one end of the hallway and paced towards each other, ending up at the entrance to their typing room. A pair of men walked by while they were doing this and didn't even say hello.

"Is it a rat in the air vent?" Sylvia wondered. The smell was clearly strongest right in their space, though the hall wasn't very pleasant either. Sylvia didn't have much experience with rats, though one apartment she'd lived in when Jordan was little had mice in the cabinets.

Sylvia went back to typing, while Marina grabbed her purse and took off. She came back forty minutes later with a plug-in scent diffuser. There wasn't a central place to put it, so Marina kindly stuck it in the outlet on Sylvia's side. "Not one night for all the time I was there passed without me seeing, hearing, or feeling what was happening to me," Sylvia typed.

The sweet magnolia was even worse than the smell of the room by itself. Her head pounded. "Let's try it on your side," Sylvia suggested. She took two ibuprofen while Marina rearranged her cords to clear a spot for the diffuser.

Over the next few days the typists took turns bringing in other brands of scent diffuser, an odor-grabbing sprinkle for the carpet, and a room spray that was supposed to have no smell of its own but would neutralize whatever was already in the air.

"We're spending our own money for this," Marina grumbled. She wanted to bring it up with Alex again, but Sylvia didn't want to.

"Well, he's the building manager. Let him manage something!" Marina said.

"Is he the building manager?" They more or less had to get used to the smell. Because it was getting worse, Sylvia believed it would go away soon. It had reached its maximum and would clear up quickly, probably over the weekend.

At the word "weekend," Marina lit up. She didn't say anything, but sat up straighter in her chair and tilted her head back. She stayed in this reverie posture long enough that Sylvia surmised she was supposed to ask what fun plans Marina had for Saturday. Sylvia didn't ask. She didn't want to know.

"It's great being in love," Marina said before Sylvia could pull the headphones back on and block news of Mr. Right.

"They took a little break and then they started kicking me very hard with their feet until I passed out," Sylvia typed. She worked for about another hour, then took two more ibuprofen.

Ink

The printer ink we call toner dates back to 1959. The Xerox company debuted a mammoth machine, the 914, that could copy documents laid across it. Its dry, particulate ink lay deep in its innards in a metal bottle. When the contraption came to life, it gulped at the document on its screen and composed a duplicate, mixing the toner with a developing fluid and collecting the waste product in yet another bottle. The 914's early adopters must have been very brave. When the toner ran out, they called a technician, who came over with a dust mask and a fire extinguisher. The powdered toner could ignite if not handled properly. I imagine Sylvia and Marina might have watched from the corner of the next room if this technician had arrived in all his gear at their workplace. It was definitely a man's job, to wrangle the machinery. More likely, the female typists of that era would have quit whatever jobs they had and stayed home with their kids. The entire operation of installing, testing, using, and then changing the toner on this landmark machine may have been witnessed only by men, unmarried young ladies, and the occasional older spinster. Of course, just because my research didn't turn up a valiant woman engineer or scientist behind the invention of toner doesn't mean that there wasn't one. There may have been several.

It might be important to insist here that there's a difference between ink and toner. We would have to look at complicated diagrams to understand how ink is squeezed out of minute nozzles in one model of printer, while in another the particulate toner latches onto a metal drum and all the black dust then falls away except those magnetized dots that cling to the impressions of words. I'm sure I could walk into an Office Depot and find a man who would stand in the aisle patiently explaining all this to me. Even if he knew nothing more about it than what he had in a PDF of a brochure from one of the manufacturers, he'd take his time to read it out verbatim to me, with asides for explaining electricity and the difference between positive and negative charges.

Today's printer ink, I'm told, is 98 percent water, but is nevertheless unbelievably expensive ounce for ounce. The pressure under which it's shot out within the tight confines of the inkjet nozzles is the equivalent of what a submarine endures when it dives below polar ice. You'd think ink was positively suffering as it breaks into its microdroplets, each cascading into the next to form lines and squiggles, such as the letter *r* within the word *room* within a phrase I've now repeated several times. Toner, on the other hand, is ground from black plastic. Infused with heat, it melts itself together onto the page, creating forms first dreamed of within brains and given shape by mouths and fingers. It doesn't care what it says. It follows the electrostatic outlines on the page, and can do no different. Toner does not use water. Its process is controlled by fire, or fire's controlled derivatives. Most people will not have thought about the implications, the almost astrological distinction between printing a document on an inkjet printer and copying a few smeary pages on a hulking, overheated laser printer.

The circuitous way I go about explaining the nature of ink, with my tangential progress and stops for Sylvia and Marina, bloodhounds, and the view out my window, would frustrate this man in the Office Depot as much as he frustrates me. That's not how to tell it, he might think. He might focus on the price and the efficiency of the printer he presumes I want to buy. There must be some advantages to one model over the other. "What's that little lady up to?" he might say to his buddy. "Not exactly a serious customer, I should have known."

Sunnier

After the blustery day of the show choir fund-raiser car wash, the weather took a turn towards warmer and brighter. After four straight days of this, Marina came into work in a beige trench coat with short puffed sleeves and a long gold-buckled belt that swung against her calves. It was more a decoration than a real outer garment, perfect for days when you could go without a coat but wanted to wear one. She laid it over the back of her chair and stuffed her purse in the bottom drawer. "I'm so sorry," she told Sylvia. "You're not going to believe this."

Sylvia put the headphones down around her neck. She released the pedal so the sentence "He grabbed my head and hit it against the wall and then tied my hands . . ." was left incomplete. Marina told her that she had changed out her purse because it was so warm. She assumed that Sylvia had gotten a good glimpse of her seasonally appropriate bag, but Sylvia had only had eyes for the coat.

"I took everything out of the old one, you know, and what's crammed in the bottom in a plastic bag but one of Jayda's little undies all sopped with pee. Oh my god, I've been carrying that around for weeks. No wonder it smells in here."

Today she was carrying a fresh purse, completely clean, not even any old kleenex balled up in it.

The women typed. The room had no windows, but the air was still a little different, maybe just moister, with the warm, sunny day outside.

"How's Jayda doing?" Sylvia asked. "She still peeing in school?"

"I'm taking her to the doctor. Of course that makes it worse. She had a fit about it. But who knows, it could be an infection."

"What about her green phobia?"

"Mmmm . . ." Marina said. She shook her head and looked down at her keyboard. Sylvia thought she wasn't going to get an answer, and kept on typing. She missed part of Marina's explanation, which seemed to be what Ted thought of Jayda's problems. Sylvia had to push herself to recall who Ted was. Mr. Right. Sylvia didn't see how he could have an opinion on Jayda. Marina hadn't known him very long. It seemed like he thought the little girl was trying to get attention and they should ignore her.

"Does he have kids?"

"He loves kids."

Marina smiled, and Sylvia thought she might have missed telling Marina that her haircut looked nice. Was it shorter, or just wavier in the humidity? She didn't want to risk the comment, and it was too late now anyway.

By the afternoon it was clear to Sylvia that the sub-odor of urine hadn't left the room. It couldn't have been due to Jayda's undies. She got a little tube of highly scented hand lotion out of her desk drawer and put that on. She took two ibuprofen, washing them down with a Sprite she bought from the vending machine in the break room. She climbed the stairs to the third floor, used that bathroom though the soap was the same as in all the other dispensers, and walked down the stairs at the other end of the hallway. She passed some women lugging files and clipboards. They didn't look at her but said to each other, "Two Oh Eight?" "Two Oh Eight."

She went outside to the smoke break bench. No one was sitting there, though the metal can for the butts released a thin plume from something left smoldering just moments ago. Gardeners had dug up a flower bed. The earth stood in two stiff rows, ready for plants to be pushed down into it. A scraggly bush on the other end leaned over, heavy with pink buds. It was so warm that sweat ran down Sylvia's legs, released from behind her knees and dampening her nylons. She looked down at her shoes, the same ones she'd worn yesterday. She hadn't made the shift to sandals yet. She should probably dig her sandals out of the closet when she went home tonight.

Mute Objects of Expression

The poet Ponge didn't let his compositions rest, but wrote the same phrase with minute variations in succeeding paragraphs, producing many similar but imperfect versions. He fiddled with the placement of the conjunctions or changed the word order, no one iteration the precise string of words he wanted. A poem from 1940, when he was still an unknown insurance agent and not yet "the poet Ponge," describes a pinewoods. In their summer aspect, the woods are "a pavilion of aromatic hairpins." A few pages later, he's got "a resilient layer of aromatic hairpins." Then, "on a deep, resilient ground of aromatic hairpins" something rises, tools or toadstools. He tries to turn the August woods into a kind of beauty parlor, with mirrors and brushes, though in the same woods he also sees the sturdy handles of manly implements. He struggles to be clear, never saying that broken-off branches lie around *like* discarded loppers and shovels. He doesn't use simile, this is like that, or like this. His specificity plods and stumbles. He wants the woods themselves to manifest concretely, but words intrude. The words too become objects. His phrases plead to the reader, smiling shyly from his page: pick me, choose me.

Ponge must have thought himself a buffoon, especially compared to gallant poets who laid down their choicest language in neat lines adorned with rhyme, alliteration, and clever allusion. Lord Byron, for example, who gave us his little bit from *Don Juan* about the power of a drop of ink to make millions think, would hardly have committed his missteps to publication. Ponge on the other hand starts a line with dashes, then repeats the same line with one word different, introduced this time with three dots. He caps the paragraph with the abbreviation *Var.* and sets down the line again with yet another tweak.

He seems to have expected the reader's patience, the way kids endure their mom's sisters' friends at an annual holiday dinner. He could easily have cleaned up his paragraphs, excised the variants that weren't the best, and made a final choice. Instead he let his readers see his ineffectual progress and eventual defeat.

His masterpiece "Soap" lay fallow for years between its drafts, and he only finalized it when he read it on the radio in Germany in 1964. It didn't make any sense for the French poet to at last release "Soap" on German airwaves. When he started the piece, the blathering of a little bar of soap might have harked back to the confessions of prisoners captured by the Nazis and their collaborators. By 1964, everyone had forgotten all that and had built new buildings and train lines. "Soap" evolved into a kind of amnesia.

When he finally published "Soap," he put Camus's critical letter right in the middle of the first, earliest section. Camus advised Ponge to tighten up "Soap" a bit. The master was baffled by it. He was being kind, but clearly he didn't think the poem was very good. Ponge's "Soap," over its long gestation, is a record of ridiculousness, of how vain the poet's effort is, how inevitable our failure when we try to say what a thing is. "Wasn't there something . . . ?" he wrote, trying to recall the impulse of the younger Ponge who had started the piece.

Sylvia couldn't go back to ask Alex about the hand soap in the Ladies anymore. She was done talking to him. When he came in to mess around in the supply cabinet or to pick up their folders, she kept the headphones on. If she made eye contact with him by accident, she pretended that she hadn't. She released the pedal that ran the tape machine and listened to the roar it left. Sometimes the translator paused between phrases, and she thought he was done speaking or that the tape was messed up. No telling whether it was a mechanical difficulty or a hesitation. As if maybe the translator . . .

But then he revved up again. "After that they took me to a closed room and more than 5 guards poured water on me."

Sylvia stared at Alex while pretending not to see him. He didn't react. He didn't care enough about her to see the loss of her esteem as an injury to himself. He bent over and got some little boxes out of the bottom shelf, probably binder clips.

"You're not the building manager," she said to him. She was still inside the hissing headphones, and she couldn't hear her own voice. He didn't answer, but his mouth drooped open. Then it moved up and down, forming words. Sylvia took the headphones off.

"What?"

"Who told you I was the building manager?"

"You're always managing. We thought you were the building manager. But you're Jerome's assistant. Or whoever has Jerome's job now. You're like Clerk II or something."

"I don't even know what you're talking about," he said. He tried to turn the conversation flip and positive by inserting a fake smile. "I'm sorry," he said. "I'm sorry about the soap."

He lost the smile. It was possible he really meant it. She buried herself in the typewriter. "After that they beat me with a broom and . . ." The air moved, signaling the opening and shutting of the door to the corridor. She didn't know why she wanted to make an enemy out of someone as harmless as Alex. She was really lowering herself. The napkins on the top of the file cabinet lifted, then settled. The air current from the door wasn't strong enough to move the wooden coffee stirrers. The stirrers lay sullenly across the napkins, not caring what happened to them.

Show Choir Costume III

Jordan came with her only reluctantly. He had stuff to do, though all Sylvia witnessed him doing was mooning over a video game, starting it over and over again as his character fell onto pitchforks from high rooftops or stumbled into booby-trapped barrels or open sewers. He swore and pounded his leg, all directed at the screen and so nothing for Sylvia to take offense at. She wondered why he played the game if it was so exasperating. She prodded him four or five times before he roused himself and stomped out the door behind her, his shoelaces flapping.

"Close the door, Jordan!" she said. He got out of the car and went back and shut the front door.

"Did you lock it?"

He got out again to go back inside and twist the knob in the handle. He had his own key and could have locked the deadbolt like his mother always did, but he couldn't be bothered. Sylvia had to let that go. The route to the formal wear rental store took them to the farthest edges of mall land. She took a wrong turn and had to double back, taking a perilous left turn over three lanes of traffic. Jordan didn't notice, so he couldn't accuse her of getting lost and wasting his time. She asked him to look out the window and try to spot the place, because it was on his side. He turned his head and stayed glued to the passing storefronts, which on her side of the road were a mattress superstore, a tire mart, a drive-through coffee place, a tax accountant, and a day care.

"It's up there," he said.

"Where?"

"There. See the sign? Mom, turn. Turn, Mom, turn!"

She got herself into the parking lot one strip mall over from where she wanted to be, and there was no driveway connecting the two. She parked anyway, and she and Jordan walked over a weedy grass bumper to get into the right parking lot. Jordan lagged behind, and she was first into the little shop, bells jangling as the door swung open. A wrinkled man, Indian or Pakistani, fussed over Jordan. Jordan stood on a little rug, enduring the man stooping and circling with the measuring tape. Sylvia thought he minded her watching, so she went to the window and fingered the neckties hanging from a rack.

She turned around when Jordan came out of the dressing room in the suit. He smiled at her over his shoulder as he adjusted to get a glimpse of himself from the back. Sylvia held in any words. In the serious gray garb he looked taller and older, the kid replaced by a dashing man. The shrouded light of the little store softened his acne. He looked pleased with his reflection. Without the habitual scowl he wore at home, his features came into better alignment.

The storekeeper put Jordan's arms through several positions and made suggestions about the cuffs. They talked about the occasion.

"You're a singer? Very nice," the man said. "See how it is to take a bow."

Jordan swept forward, his arm on his chest, and lifted. He and the man conferred over whether it wasn't too tight in the shoulders. Jordan agreed to try a slightly larger jacket, so he had room to move. A jacket for standing and looking nice and a jacket for a performer were two different things, the man explained. The store proprietor wanted to be sure he rented Jordan a jacket he could move freely in. "No dancing, then? Just singing?"

"A few steps," Jordan said. He demonstrated, floating left and right, chin high, arms out.

"What does Mom say?" the man asked, after Jordan tried the second jacket. Jordan fixed his eyes on her.

She turned back to the rack of neckties. Jordan came up behind her and put his arms around her. She felt her shoulders droop as his warmth ran down her back. She reached around and patted his hand.

"Always emotional for the moms, to see the little boy grown up," the proprietor said. Sylvia sniffed loudly, and Jordan stepped back. She turned around and engaged the man about the terms. She avoided his eyes while asking him when it had to be back, the deposit, the hanger and covering plastic sheath. She handed him her debit card. He slid it through the machine himself, turning it over and examining her signature.

He printed out the contract. She stood with the page in her hand, face tilted towards it. She posed as if she could really read the print, but she was just making a show. She couldn't keep the tears from coming. The lines of type moved, swimming in the water brimming her eyes. She wiped the tears away with the back of her hand. Jordan hovered behind her. She felt his shadow, as if he had just that moment become his four inches taller than her.

She didn't know how she was going to get out of there, and was grateful for Jordan's continued small talk with the proprietor. He told the man some things about his rehearsal schedule that she hadn't known.

"We're performing at Disneyland in May," he added.

The check for the trip had been due last week. Sylvia remembered where the form was, in the pile on the kitchen counter. The realization that she'd screwed that up drained her sentimental stewing. She decided to turn the money and form in by hand at the school office on her way to work tomorrow, and not mention it to Jordan. She cleared her throat and lifted from her swampy focus on the rental contract.

"We need to stop at the store and get some bread," she said to Jordan, cutting off his conversation with the man.

She couldn't see his face because he was behind her, but from the way he dragged his feet, his expression had probably reverted to his sullen hurtfulness.

He hung the suit on a hook by the back passenger window that she'd never known was there. Many times she'd seen people driving with their dry cleaning flapping. She was afraid it would foul her sight line for turning out of the lot, but she was fine.

Ink

I thought I had come to the end of things to say about ink, until I found a note to myself yesterday that reminded me about its capacity for corrosion. The ink that was made for dipping quill pens was of varying quality. Some was dark but turned lighter, some was brownish but turned blacker. Some of this handmade ink got clogged with particles or came out so runny it had to be set out in the sun to evaporate. For all its faults, this ink coexisted kindly with the quill.

The makers of steel pens thought they had a huge improvement. No more men sitting on the banks of ponds pulling the stout wing feathers from geese. The nineteenth-century English steel pen, with its metal nib cut with three little slices to direct the ink, lasted longer than a quill and felt sturdier in the hand. It was better suited for men and business. The writer dipped it into the inkwell and heard a satisfying clink. This sound accompanied the flow and interruption of the writer's thought.

But the inks that had worked well in quill pens ate away at the steel nib. Even with careful cleaning, the steel pens eventually turned into corroded monsters, writing wide, uneven scraggles. The precise incisions that sent the ink from the nib onto the page opened into uneven rifts. The ink flowed down the degraded metal unchecked. Instead of making loops and lines, the ink formed blots. The writer using a corroded pen ultimately blocked out words rather than shaped them. The writer may have risen from her desk a disaster of blackened hands. She left her fingerprints up and down the edges of a page of halting blobs. Uncontrolled lines connected these splats, where here and there an *a* or *m* peeked out. The writer looked down at this mess and decided to throw out the instrument that had promised so much when new. It took a steady hand and diligent wiping and soaking to keep steel pens in shape. No matter what, the ink ultimately had its way and ripped the pen apart.

The pen makers blamed the ink makers for the destruction of their instruments. The pen makers branched out and began making their own inks, specified for use with their pens. Ink's ideal qualities are described like this: "It must run freely, but not spread; it should not smell, or be liable to go bad; it should dry easily; it should not harm the paper on which it is used." And of course, it should not harm the writing instrument. In actuality, ink of that era ate away at paper and was capable of dissolving the nib that laid it down. This is a challenge we've totally forgotten about.

It's so peaceful to write on my laptop, where the words appear as figments of themselves on a portrait of a white page, and the wrong, misplaced words and phrases can be undone with just the push of the Backspace key. It's all so clean. I've at times dissolved whole manuscripts by clicking on the file name and pressing Delete. If I change my mind about a word, I highlight it and type something else in its place. In this way, I don't even have to erase. Just eradicate.

The other day I had to ask for a morning off work to take my car to get its brakes fixed. I brought the whole folder of pages of this very novel with me. I sat in the plastic bucket seat at Car-X, reading through and making notes, *delete this, move this. What is this?* I filled the nice white paper with my stern editorial injunctions, crossing through lines and writing in small script what seemed to be a better sentiment. The model tires mounted on the walls infused the waiting room with a strong rubbery smell, overridden by the tang of a Mr. Coffee pot burning on its heated ring.

A man came in and took a seat 90 degrees from me. He thumbed through the men's magazines that I usually enjoy reading in the Car-X waiting room. I didn't know men had these worries about their prostate and being stuck in the "friend zone," and I like stories about rock climbing. I kept on fluffing through my loose manuscript pages, scritching with my pen while he read the magazines. After a while, I realized the man's eyes were on me.

He'd never think I'm writing a novel, I thought. Even if I could explain it to him—two women typing unbearable transcripts of detained men at Abu Ghraib, and some things that happen to them, and some other things—his eyes would glaze over. Is it a mystery? he might ask. A romance? Then he would tell me about some friend of his who wrote something once, without any more questions for me.

It would be easier to pass myself off as a crazy person obsessing over a memoir of her schizophrenia or an accusation against a lover who wronged her. Real writers, I'm sure this man getting his car serviced would think, don't sit in Car-X with pages strewn over the stained side table. They don't make that uncomfortable noise with the drying point of the Staedtler Triplus Fineliner that I prefer for editing. Crazy people stare at their pages and make marks on them, not letting the pages rest. To fidget over the exact right word probably seemed like a weakness. And I had so many pages with me, over a hundred at that point. They spilled out of their folder and occupied the whole tabletop. They were an embarrassment.

I didn't try to explain myself. I turned my attention back to my task. I crossed out "some" and wrote "a" or "the." I took out commas, then put them back again in the same spot. I weighed the placement of paragraphs and drew arrows sending them back or forward. If a note on a quarter sheet of scrap paper slid to the floor, and it said on it in green cursive, "5 different weights of font, from black to gray, book to light," I didn't worry what the man in the Car-X would make of it. I felt very good about this interaction, or lack of one. I felt it was a real victory.

Blood III

Marina kept getting up and going out. Sylvia huddled in the headphones, and it shouldn't have mattered to her. They were each in their own little world. "I was there for 67 days of suffering and little to eat," she typed. She took a break herself, by sitting still and letting the hiss of the tape stretch on. The machine exhaled in her ear with the foot pedal on pause. Sylvia's fingers touched the keys of the typewriter in the ready position, thumbs hovering over the space bar, the *g* and *h* looking back at her from the center of the console. These were the silent letters in *light* and *night*, so they said nothing. A blankness in the middle. The gap between words.

Marina came back in with a bottle of ibuprofen in her hand. Sylvia slipped off the headphones and caught the clink of Marina setting the bottle down firmly on her desk ledge, making a point of it. Sylvia started to say something, but Marina didn't meet her eyes. Marina seemed to be going at her typing with gusto now. Sylvia put a few words down, then let the pause take over again. She didn't really feel like doing anything this morning. She fiddled with a hangnail, then searched the backs of her desk drawers, looking for a mint or a cough drop.

"Oh my god," Marina said, a couple times until Sylvia engaged.

"What?"

"I had like a super tampon in and it's done already. I can't take this anymore. Do you have any?"

"Any tampons?"

"Any big ones. I bought one in the machine and it's tiny. Or regular."

Sylvia dug through the pouch in her purse. Marina came over to look at what she had. Sylvia laid the headphones down and made space for her bag on the desk. Marina wasn't happy at the thin pink plastic things Sylvia drew out. Sylvia offered to get in her car and go get her some supers. She owed Marina a trip to the drugstore, for the day Marina had fetched the plug-in scent diffuser.

"I'll deal," Marina said. She limped back to her desk. A thin line of red ran down the inside of one leg, reaching almost to her shoe.

"I think you might need to change," Sylvia said.

Marina had already sat back down. Sylvia had to get up and go tell her to her face. Marina sprang up, and the two of them stared down at the stain on the chair seat. It was really only a little one, though the back of Marina's skirt was worse. "I can feel it like waves," she said. "It's not normal."

Sylvia had times like that too, she said, but they discussed whether it could be a miscarriage or something. Marina considered some dates, and remembered a friend of hers who had fibroids. "I'm probably okay," Marina said. "It's nothing. Just nature's revenge."

She took herself off to the Ladies to clean up. She came back bare legged. She had thrown her nylons away. Blood stained the rim of one shoe, but Sylvia said no one would notice. They used the napkins off the top of the filing cabinet to blot Marina's chair. She tied her blazer around her waist by the sleeves to hide the vulval shape imprinted on her skirt. The sleeveless blouse she had on under the blazer gapped badly between the buttons.

Alex came in just as Sylvia was walking across the room with the wad of bloody napkins. He dropped his eyes from her face to the mess in her hands, his mouth open. He swiveled, looking to retreat, while still stepping towards Marina's desk. He looked so terrified that Sylvia laughed. Marina turned pink all the way down to the tops of her breasts, visible above the last button of the skimpy shirt. Marina said nothing to him, proffering her closed folder with one hand while with the other drawing the heavy headphones back on. Sylvia stood where she was, halfway to the trash can. Alex took the folder and stuffed the typed forms more neatly down into it. He might have been able to read a few lines from the top or bottom of the casually enclosed transcripts, such as "They brought 6 people and beat me until I dropped to the floor."

"Thanks, Marina," he said. It came out in a half whisper. His saying her name meant he pointedly wasn't saying Sylvia's name. He might have seen at a glance that there wasn't anything in her folder yet anyway. She'd hardly done any work this morning.

Marina complained mid-afternoon that she felt like she was wearing a diaper. She'd gone to the tampon-plus-pad combo to deal with her overflow. The ibuprofen seemed to have kicked in, though. "When they torture me they took gloves and they beat my dick and testicles," Sylvia typed. That was about enough for that day.

Jayda

One morning Marina came in late, grimly towing her little daughter. She sat Jayda on the floor in the center of the room with a coloring book and a pencil case of markers. Jayda scribbled listlessly, glancing over often at her mom's feet working the pedal on the Dictaphone. Sylvia couldn't get her to say much besides "hi." She squatted down next to her and said she'd seen Jayda's picture and was pleased to meet her, but it didn't go over. Jayda hunched over the the book and wouldn't speak.

Marina didn't say what was going on, so it was obviously something she couldn't talk about in front of her daughter. She gave Sylvia an eloquent look when they were both in their headphones. Sylvia couldn't interpret it. She observed the little girl's long, matted hair and neat, sockless ankles. Jayda smelled a little bit, the ripeness of unwashed clothes, adding to the general odor of the room where Sylvia and Marina typed. Sylvia craned her neck to look over at the oil infuser plugged in by the base of Marina's desk. It might be that those things needed to be changed once a month. Sylvia put her chin in her hands thoughtfully, and yanked back from the stench on her fingertips. It was probably powdered cheese reacting with hand sanitizer, but even the plain water in the Ladies taps now seemed to have a pee-pee whiff. It was impossible to know where it was coming from.

Bruce, Jayda's dad, was supposed to come for her at lunchtime. At noon Marina marched the girl out of the room. She began shrieking at the doorway and clawing at the knob. "Why can't I stay with you?" she wailed.

Marina's voice went very low, calm and stern. "Daddy's taking you for ice cream," she admonished.

The door closed behind them, but Sylvia heard the child's sobs take up again. After a few minutes Sylvia went out and asked Marina if there was anything she could do.

Marina leaned over the little girl, who had sprawled on the linoleum in a mass of tears and snot. She was crying so hard, Sylvia worried she'd pass out. Every now and then she took a shuddering inhale, but it didn't seem like enough. Marina talked to her low and urgently, looking down and over Jayda's head. Marina cocked her head up and in the same quiet, earnest tone asked Sylvia to go out to the parking lot and see if she could bring Jayda's dad down.

Sylvia didn't see any man loitering near the back entrance, so she peered in car windows. Then she spotted a gray Taurus idling by the curb behind her. It was the only car not actually parked in a slot. She felt stupid for not realizing earlier that this had to be Bruce's car. She knocked on the window. The genial smiler was indeed Bruce, Marina's ex.

"Jayda's having a major meltdown, and Marina asked me to come get you," Sylvia said.

"I'm gonna find that guy and kill him," Bruce said.

Sylvia gave him a hard look. Bruce was still smiling, though only small and tight around the lips. All through showing her badge to the security guard and turning the corner and going down the stairs, Sylvia wondered what to say. It was better not to ask, if something was really wrong. She knew Jayda was sensitive, and had that weird phobia of green, and other things. Maybe she was always like this. Just before turning into the hall that led to the typing room, she pushed it out anyway: "Do you mean the guy she's dating?"

Bruce didn't answer, but started to run when they heard an outburst from Jayda. Bruce stooped over where she lay bawling on the floor and grabbed her up. The child's legs kicked and arms waved like some kind of spider, her limbs seeming to extend from the man's torso. Audrey and Georgia had come out of their office and stood outside it, watching the commotion. Bruce lurched towards the stairs, murmuring, "Hush, baby, hush." Marina walked behind them, one hand holding a hank of

Jayda's hair. Though Sylvia couldn't make out the words, the low, serious stream of sentences continued to pour out of Marina. Bruce's soothing words and Marina's burble gradually diminished as the trio rounded the corner. Jayda's wail kept on until it was blocked by a closing door.

Sylvia stepped quickly back into the office and sat herself down. She pulled the headphones on and listened to the harsh, unmodulated breath of the tape on pause. When Marina came in, Sylvia didn't look up. Keeping her head down to the keyboard, she tried to get a glimpse of Marina through her lashes. She raised her head a little when Marina walked around her desk and turned her back. Sylvia got a glimpse of raccoon-like mascara as Marina returned to her seat.

"Will she be okay?" Sylvia asked.

"God knows," Marina answered. "Bruce settled her down for now. I don't know what I'm going to do."

They both went back under the headphones. About twenty minutes later they took a little break, and Marina told Sylvia the whole story.

Show Choir Concert

Sylvia kept herself back from telling Jordan not to stuff the rented suit into his backpack, though he would have seen it in her face if he looked her way. Her son studiously kept his expression neutral and turned away from hers as he banged out the door. "Wait!" she called after him. The high school was so huge and confusing, she wouldn't find the auditorium unless he reminded her which door to go in. He was already gone, and she knew it was Door 4 anyway, the one with the mural.

She walked through Door 4 that night just as Parrish's parents were arriving, and Parrish too. They found good seats near the front. Parrish's mom slid over to talk to another mom. This woman greeted Sylvia, saying Jordan was such a great kid.

"Thank you," Sylvia said. She couldn't remember this woman's daughter's name, so she didn't say anything else. She talked to Parrish's dad about traffic. She couldn't believe her good fortune, that she'd gotten to the concert on time. It would be longer to sit on the uncomfortable seats, Parrish's dad said. He'd heard the school was going to raise money to replace them. Sylvia didn't know anything about that. "Great!" she said. It would probably not happen until after their kids graduated, though, Parrish's dad explained.

"I don't like to think about that," Sylvia said.

The auditorium filled, first with parents, then with kids in groups of five and six. Parrish's dad, at the behest of his wife, jumped up to get them all programs. They had neglected to take them off the music stand up front, and the folded sheets were almost all gone before they realized. Sylvia looked at Jordan's name in print, not her last name but his dad's.

Two whole choirs had to sing half a dozen pieces each before they got to Jordan's show choir. Sylvia mostly kept her eyes on the program, moving her thumb down the list of songs to keep track of where they were at. Marina's revelation had left her numb. She hadn't known what to say except "Oh my god" and "I'm so sorry." Marina was much more fluid with her emotions, crying and laughing and wiping her eyes, at one point accidentally and then deliberately tearing apart one of the finished transcript forms. She was drinking Pepsi because she hadn't slept or eaten and it was all she could tolerate. Her moving hands, illustrating her tale, knocked over the can and spilled brown drink onto the folder of completed documents. "This day's work is ruined," she said, showing Sylvia the soiled and wrinkled pages. Some of the typed words showed through: "they removed all my clothes down to naked for seven days."

"But, Marina, what are you going to do?"

"What can I do? What would you do? I don't even know anything happened. He didn't touch her. I don't even know if it's a crime."

Marina threw the stained transcript in the trash.

"I don't think you can do that," Sylvia said. She hovered by Marina's side. The oil diffuser blasted its lilac-lavender balm. You could only really smell it right here.

"Fuck it," Marina said, pulling the damaged triplicate pages out and stuffing them in the back of the folder. She ripped another one along the top. She didn't seem to know she was doing it. The three pages, the white and the yellow and the green, were now loosed from their binding strip.

"You can call the police and tell them. He can't get away with that."

"What am I supposed to say? Did I know what was going on? Did I let him? Where did I meet him? How long have I known him? That's what they'll want to know. God. I thought he was so romantic. He was really into me. He was so, I don't know, he was confident. I thought I'd lucked out. I mean, he was erotic down to his bones."

He had in fact paid Jayda a dollar to peek out her bedroom door and watch while he fucked her mom on the couch.

Marina kept on nervously shredding the documents in the folder. The white strips fluttered to the floor.

"Oh my god. I'm so sorry. Oh my god," Sylvia said.

Marina set the folder down, back into the puddle of Pepsi. Sylvia looked around for something to wipe up with, but they'd used up their total napkin supply on the menstrual blood the other day.

"I just," Marina went on, now taking a tack out of her cork board and pushing it back in, "I just wanted something light, you know. I mean, he was so fun, so wild. It just felt great, like, at long last, after all these losers. He wanted to move in with me. I was figuring out how to make room on the counter for his coffee maker he was going to bring."

Sylvia stayed where she was, awkwardly planted. Marina seemed to get more lighthearted momentarily, laughing at herself. "I called him Mr. Right," Marina said.

"I know. Well, you're really lucky you didn't get that far, him moving in."

"Jayda didn't see anything. I'm sure she's fine. She's just upset. She's super sensitive."

"Was this the only time?"

"She says he gave her a dollar and told her to stay awake and come to the door. She says just one time. I asked her. I'm sure it was only once, and she didn't see anything. I mean, we were . . . if she'd waited, but she didn't see anything. It was just one time, and I found out about it right away."

The more Marina repeated that it was only once, the more it seemed to Sylvia that her workmate was calculating back to some other suspicious occasions. Marina kept her face to the bulletin board, playing with the tack. Her fingers moved slowly, pushing it in and wiggling it out. She stiffened up, then burst out with another cry that was a lot like Jayda's. She stifled her sobs immediately and wiped her nose on her sleeve. She launched into a string of nasty expressions about Ted. "I don't get it," she finished. "He was so great."

Sylvia reached over and put her hand on Marina's shoulder. Marina slumped under the touch.

"Gus is okay," Marina whispered. "He has no clue. He's too little. He sleeps through everything."

"That's good," Sylvia said. She stepped back. Marina's face stayed frozen, maybe fixed on an inner film strip of her lover undressing her in various spots around the house.

"Believe you me, Jayda is enjoying the attention," Marina said. "I mean, I know she's upset, but she's taking it for all she can get."

The junior choir finished a medley of uplifting spirituals, and then a bevy of students in black sweatshirts came out to disassemble the risers. When the show choir came out, all Sylvia saw of her son was a blob of face. He was way in back. The girls looked glorious in short sequined dresses of various shades. The boys, only four of them, all had the gray suits and red vests. Jordan's was a different shade of gray, but it wasn't too noticeable.

Sylvia tried to remember the song as it was being sung, rehearsing what she would say to Jordan about it. The music didn't penetrate, however. She still kept her thumb on the program to be sure where they were at. When Parrish's dad poked her arm, she didn't know why. She thought she had done something. Words she might have said to Marina went through her mind, an alternative conversation where Marina relied on Sylvia's righteous anger and sound advice. "Are you sure it was just the one time?"

"She said it was just this once. He gave her a dollar to look out her door. Now I know why he liked it on the couch so much."

"He can't get away with this."

"What can I do?"

Sylvia would have liked to say exactly what Marina should do. She moved her arm off the rest to get away from Parrish's dad. They were four measures into the song before she realized that she was looking at Jordan, head cast down, the spotlight making a brown blur of his hair. The rest of the choir was massed behind him, and the tall girl from the car wash was at the piano.

Jordan's Song

The piano intro was very familiar. It was the tragic song Jordan played every day in his room, and that Sylvia had also heard out car windows and maybe in her own car when Jordan had his music on. The girls with the boom box at the car wash had played it. This song was everywhere. Sylvia had heard it a million times. It was that sad teen anthem that all the kids loved. Their young show choir director had acceded to the kids' request and let them sing it in their own arrangement.

While this had been explained from the stage, Sylvia's mind was filled with such a complete replica of her encounter with Marina that she hadn't taken any of it in. She had to look at her hand on the program to find herself in the auditorium. While Jordan sang, she said to herself, Jordan is singing. She looked at his lean gray figure under the spotlight, his hands on the mic blocking his mouth, yet a thick interface of the scene in that other room obtruded. Sylvia watched Jordan through a projection of Marina's face all dirty with her makeup, and her hands tearing the binding strips off the transcription forms. The smell of the room, its ammoniac fug suffused with fake floral, and the sound of the hissing breath on the tape worked itself between Sylvia and the spectacle of her son onstage.

Jordan mumbled the opening verse into the microphone, his voice husky, a little grating and unsure. The piano was too loud, or he was too soft, the words not comprehensible. The choir behind him swayed gently, barely moving, all their eyes on their soloist, not the audience.

The tape hissed, and then the dry, uninflected voice took up its tale: "He took me into the shower and stripped me naked. . . ." Sylvia's fingers struck the keys, and the typewriter clacked. "He took me into the shower and stripped me naked. He said he would come inside and rape me," said the voice, and the keys tap-tapped. Sylvia watched her son's face, now revealed as he dropped his hands from the mic. He spread his arms, opening his chest, and bawled out the only coherent lines in the song: A statement. Something she couldn't catch. A question. A statement. And a pause.

The girls in their sparkly dresses stepped forward. Their hems swung as their knees came up. They took up the next verse, continuing to move slowly forward as they sang. The other boys, their suits several shades darker and tighter fitting than Jordan's, came up between them. The show choir formed a horseshoe around Jordan. Now Sylvia couldn't make out his voice among them. She looked at the girls' white throats, all exposed as they sang, chins up. Their knees shone beneath their fluffy hems, rounded and perfect.

As they came to the chorus the next time, with its few words she could understand, Sylvia felt as if a spear had hit her chest. Heat spread from the sharp point, rushing up her neck to her face. Water streamed out of her eyes. She felt pinned to the seat by the blade, paralyzed and yet totally liquid. Her mouth opened and she found herself crying as hard as Jayda on the floor, but silently. The tears burned her eyes, sharp and chemical. The blade in her chest was so painful she put her hand there to make sure she hadn't somehow been actually shot or stabbed. The hand pressed on her sternum. Fiery rivulets ran down her spine and into her ribs and kidneys. Her face felt like it would lift off, tearing itself away from her cheekbones. At the same time, her back was bolted to the hard plastic seat, seemingly pushed back by the spike in her chest.

Jordan floated left and right, the spare dance moves she had seen him make in the formal-wear rental shop. He came to a rest in front of the microphone and sang the third verse with the rest of the choir backing him. The girls, glorious in their short gowns, kept their faces icy hard. The boys made doleful puppy eyes. It was a really sad song. Sylvia now seemed to be watching the concert from ceiling level, her vision narrow and sharp. Her body, heaving with silent sobs, sat densely in its seat. Everything ached and stung. Yet she was very quiet.

She willed herself to gather in all that was happening in front of her, a voice inside her still telling herself, Jordan is singing now. As the last notes came, the whole choir together, the voice said, Jordan is still singing. The last seconds stretched out, and she watched them disappear. Jordan has stopped singing, the voice told her.

With the silence after, and before the applause, came a slamming sense of responsibility. This fell through her, a dense, dark gravity, like an iron planet. She had failed. She had missed everything. It was all gone.

I'm sitting in my seat, she told herself.

Her hands came up and clapped vigorously. I'm clapping, she told herself. Jordan is bowing. I'm still clapping.

Parrish's dad smiled at her, and Parrish's mom reached over and squeezed Sylvia's forearm.

The Material III

A story could begin, "They took me into a room and beat me." The story could go on, "On another occasion I was forced to lie down while MPs jumped onto my back and legs." It might continue, "In the foregoing parts of this memorandum we have demonstrated . . ." and from there, we could stop. That is, a story could begin with a statement of a condition. The story continues with an elaboration of that condition. It ends with a total disavowal of any interest in or responsibility for the condition. The story, which began as a human voice, has become a piece of evidence. It's mathematical in its importance, useful or not as it demonstrates an argument. The argument is a different story from the story of the actors within it, or so it maintains.

Sylvia got up from her desk. She set the headphones down on the mass of completed forms, pushing aside an empty single-serving cup of ice cream she had taken away from a halfhearted birthday party in the break room. Marina had taken the day off to help Bruce, her ex-husband, move. He'd been practically living with her anyway, after the thing with Jayda, and now he wanted to make it official by bringing a bunch of large, heavy boxes. Or so Marina said. They were making multiple trips to Goodwill to get rid of stuff in her basement so he could put his baseball cards down there.

Sylvia looked across the room at the unoccupied desk. Her hand groped for balance as she leaned against her desk drawers. Her fingers brushed something cold and came up with the X-Acto knife she had used to rip the box of tapes open on that first day. Its blade was still open. She turned its knob to loosen the chute the blade slid in and out on. She pulled the blade back and tightened the knob again. Some numbers drawn in black marker on the side of the knife announced its place in an inventory. Sylvia wondered if Alex had been looking for it all this time. She turned it over and looked at the scratches in its yellow paint and the rust on its tail end. She thought about placing it in one of the plastic bins in the supply cabinet, but it wasn't worth the effort. She slid it back under the papers that had hidden it before.

She had driven Jordan to the bus at five that morning, and she was tired. Jordan was on his way to Disneyland with the choir. In addition to all the money she'd paid for his food and hotel room, she'd had to go on and order the gray suit from the school's purveyor. That meant she'd wasted the money spent on the rental. She should have just knuckled under right away. At least Jordan had said thank you really sincerely, while looking at her. He gave her a hug in the parking lot before he boarded the bus, maybe because the other kids were hugging their moms too.

Sylvia sat down again and drew the warm cups of the headphones over her ears. "They took me into a room and beat me," she typed. "On another occasion I was forced to lie down while MPs jumped onto my back and legs." The voice of the translator droned on, slow and precise, emptied of inflection. It wasn't the translator's story. The translator had merely turned some sounds into other sounds, which created words in English. These sounds in English formed instructions in Sylvia's brain that moved her fingers over the keyboard. Out of this, numbered documents appeared, typed on a typewriter even though most other documents in this part of the world were created on a computer. It was a miracle, the dull open spaces of the paper converting into dense black paragraphs. Out of potential, actuality. Out of a man's legs shattered by other men jumping off a table onto him, a record.

A plastic plant looked down from the top of the filing cabinet where the napkins and coffee stirrers had lain undisturbed for months. They were all gone. Marina had brought the trailing ivy in when she was tidying up to make room for her ex to move back into her house. It was technically a Christmas decoration, but Marina had taken the red bow off it. Marina had wanted a real plant, but there was no light for it. "This is as good as we get," she said, turning it, stepping back, and moving it again until she was satisfied with the angle of its descending tendril. "On another occasion," Sylvia typed, "I was forced to lie down . . ." That is, she had already typed that line, and she typed another line very similar to it.

I had thought that at this point in the story I could simply spill ink over a couple pages. I could create a stain made of all the words I would have written, combined into one mess. One of the difficulties of writing is that the ink needs to be drawn into neat shapes in order to render letters, words, and therefore meaning. The writer has to create a fine, controlled scribble even to describe the effect of a bottle of ink spilled across a notebook. Simply spilling the ink doesn't have the impact of narrating the black puddle. The writer can't create a total blotting out with ink in order to portray the totality of the spill. The splash of ink would be illegible. For the writer's words to be legible, the writing fluid has to be controlled. If this is a mistake, then the writer doesn't have the answer. Control is evident at every instance of the narratives of the beaten men, groans of agony and rage for retribution siphoned into these precise, formal statements, with notations for time—"I was hanging there for about 5 hours"—and the exclusion of extraneous detail that might take the focus off the immediate interaction. Even the most simple sentence, "They took me into a room and beat me," is not the man, or the beating, or the beaters. Between the poles of silence and incoherent screams, the writer has stretched a hammock of neatly rendered words.

A typist doesn't have the amplitude that the writer by hand does. The writer by hand can make her letters shake, or slant, or crowd. The typist might hit the keys harder or softer, depending on her feelings, but the effect on the page is minuscule. Typewriter ink is contained by its ribbon, and the worst it can do is to smudge. When a ribbon needs changing, the type gets light. At its most distressed, it barely says anything. The writer experiences relief when she inserts a new ribbon and sees her words once again black and sure. The Selectric's ribbon never faded. It gave out after a few aberrant letters and became worthless. This caused a small interruption, where the typist changed the ribbon, actually in this instance called a cartridge.

The way I write, here on my laptop, I draw on an ever-replenishing fount of pixels. Even my shakiest draft of a letter, poem, or essay snaps dark on white on the computer's screen. My worst word choice sits there on the representation of the page with all the air of privilege of the new word that replaces it. I can backspace and substitute, for example "fount" for "source," and it makes no difference to the serene regularity of the image of the page. I'd have to provide the reader with an illustration of the horrific scrawl I made on the pages I brought with me to the Car-X that day, to get across the missteps and misalignments, the doubts and deletions, behind the fixed surface of the printed product. My notes to myself:

What was I thinking?
Move this later
Something has to happen here—Marina gets flowers?

would only clutter a narrative that's jumbled enough already.

The writer continues to be precise, and the clean surface of the page on the screen encourages the writer's confidence. I'd have to take a hammer to the machine to get the effect I want, of ink spilled into an obliterating splotch. And that wouldn't even do it. No way those pixels would come frothing out, smearing the desk and ruining everything they touched, my checkbook, pages in file folders, warranties and contracts, two love letters, pictures of the kids, old receipts, the rug I got from my mom.

Netflix IV

With Jordan away, Sylvia thought she'd relax into the quiet of the house. She put some clothes away that had lain on the back of the couch for months or longer. She had bought ingredients to cook herself pasta with broccoli that Jordan didn't like. Instead she heated up a can of soup. It was a kind of soup that neither she nor Jordan liked, and it had taken up space in the cabinet for much longer than the clothes on the couch, so eating it was a kind of victory. It was even more of a victory to pour most of it down the sink and sit on the couch with a package of stale low-fat butter cookies. Neither she nor Jordan liked these low-fat butter cookies, which is why they were still in the drawer, but they would do. She prepared to watch Netflix or some other similar streaming service. She hadn't watched anything in a long time. None of the titles were familiar. She clicked through the recommendations, reading half of the descriptions. *A woman descends into . . . Two troubled fire fighters . . . In this zany comedy, a trio of . . . Sarah thinks she's seen . . .*

She clicked on something. A man walked up to a door. The tenants let him into their living room, where they were cutting cocaine on the coffee table. Two cops conferred in their car. A teenage girl in a girly bedroom pasted a ticket into a scrapbook. Her dad said something reprehensible to her through the door. A teddy bear key chain hung off her backpack. This key chain was surely going to turn up in a dump a few minutes later.

The couch supported Sylvia's weight. Its foam had indented to accommodate her shape. At the other end, a similar hollow held itself ready for Jordan. Sylvia picked up a catalog of sprightly clothes. She flicked through ruffled skirts and lace-edged sweaters, missing all the essentials of the search for the teenage girl. These were clothes she would never wear. Whoever had sent her the catalog had no idea of her preferences. She stared at a pair of boots in a pale buff color with boxy toes. She had never had any boots remotely like these. And they were so expensive. Who did they think she was?

Her friend Carrie called to see how she was doing with Jordan away.

"Oh my god, it's so nice," Sylvia said. "I don't have to do anything!" Then she heard a little bit more about Carrie's divorce. Since she was leaving her boring husband for another man she really liked, it didn't seem so bad to Sylvia. But there were some legal complications.

"Can you believe it?" Carrie said.

"Oh my god," Sylvia said. "Look, I've got something on the stove. Thanks for calling." They made plans to see a movie. They were movie friends. Carrie had taken to cancelling at the last minute, with all she had going on, so Sylvia didn't take their date too seriously. They hadn't picked the movie or the place, or even specified Saturday or Sunday. "Okay, great, I gotta go," Sylvia said.

By that time, she had no idea what the cops were doing in the casino. They went up the stairs, guns drawn. In the veiled gray of a part of the casino under renovation, they found a dead girl. Shapely legs stuck out from under a sheet of thick, translucent plastic. One foot was bare, one was arched perfectly into a stiletto-heeled pump. The detectives stared down at this dead creature, mourning her beauty. The lead cop flicked the plastic off her face. The actress lay very still, or the camera had a way of freezing the frame so that you couldn't tell the actress was breathing. The cops shook their heads. It wasn't the girl they were looking for.

Water

On Sunday I sat down at the computer. Before I could open its lid and gaze into its facsimile of a white page, I turned my head to the right and caught a strip of dark blue. Lake Monona, first white, then gray, had shed its last ice in the morning sun and now moved slightly, just a vague undulation perceptible from this distance. All the energy that had been bound up in its static coating had let go. A rim of snow lined the far shore, and the brown field and stark trees between the near shore and my house still spoke emphatically of paralysis. The sky, filled with disconnected banks of clouds, hovered over the dark, shifting water.

I only went out on the ice once all winter. That one afternoon I ventured halfway across, when the family with their dog made it clear to me it was safe. The spring thaw meant my ability to put my body out far from shore, to trek away from the neighborhood and listen to snowflakes slicing into each other, was over for another year. Presumably it would get warmer and warmer, April sliding into May, and the perfume from lilacs and apple trees blooming together would overwhelm even the dreariest parking lot. The frozen lake presented such an opportunity for emptiness. Now that the ice had melted, I had to contend with action, with motion, with fluid possibilities. That should be a good thing. I had longed for winter to be over. But I missed it, now that it was too late to do anything about it.

I vacuumed the living room and returned some books to the library. By the time I got back to my computer, the sun was out. Here was something different again, the serious blue water replaced by a dancing shimmer. Points of sunlight reflected off the irregularities on the moving surface, sending a cascade of prisms up against my eyes. The sun off the ice had been so different, a clean sheen, not this uncapturable motion. Something that had been vast but fixed was now broken up into all its components. The water was much harder to look at than the ice. I felt uneasy. The water was so lively. It seemed to be demanding something.

The poet Ponge wrote about water in his book *The Nature of Things*. Ponge never described soap accurately, and he knew it. The bubbles as bunches of grapes, soap's worn-out aspect like a wedding guest with a hangover—he tries and tries, but always blows it. You'd almost think, reading "Soap," that Ponge was a charlatan. He clowned at being a poet, clanging his words to the ground like bowling pins. Taking a running start at his phrases, he doesn't make it. "Dear friend," he wrote, in the guise of his own reader chewing him out: "You disappoint us."

Ponge's "Water" stunned me. In just a few paragraphs, he called up an aspect of water that had never occurred to me. Water has a compulsion to go low, I read. It has a single vice: gravity. It will lie and cheat to get to the bottom. It has no scruples. It won't take form. It's anxious and obsessed. It's like an addict in the family—forever given a second chance, though totally ruled by bad habits. Water is weak willed. It's childish and easily manipulated. Ponge described how the sun exacts revenge on water. The sun organizes the cycle of heat, evaporation, and rain. In this way the sun keeps water running in circles, like a hamster on a wheel.

Ponge didn't know what to say about soap. Yet he dared to make water this abject loafer. Where he couldn't let himself get at the crimes that soap washed away, he was able to reveal water's juvenile brutality.

I tried to disagree. Water should be congratulated for being ceaseless, changing, and a murmuring speaker. It's fodder for a poet to wonder about the course of a life. Contemplation of water should bring calm. Water opens into uncontainable mystery. Earth, air, fire, and water: it's an element. It can't be mocked. Water soothes and caresses. It's a balm for the spirit. That's why I've been living by the lake. I've assumed all along that its constant transitions are meaningful.

Water is crafty, Ponge wrote. It connives. It will do anything to go downwards. Water, he wrote, is truly a slave.

It was Tuesday morning. As I was reading Ponge's "Water," I was actually passing Lake Monona, and I could see the water out of the window of the bus. I had gotten my preferred place in the back, on a seat that faces into the bus, perpendicular to the direction of travel. Often I'm left staring at the top of the head of a man enrapt in his phone, but when the opposite seats are empty, I get a good view of the lake for about half my commute to work. For these past months, I've been looking out the window at ice, a white expanse behind the white of snow and black of bare trees. But a few days after the thaw, there it was, blue and heaving. I had never thought of water as a minor gangster, ready to run off as soon as integrity was required. Water had never seemed to me like a captured rodent, foolishly racing for escape and getting nowhere. For all my reading and study, my dragging Ponge into my story of the beaten men, I'd missed this. I'd likely missed much more.

I opened my bag, which held a mess of loose typed pages, and put *The Nature of Things* back in it. I snapped it shut. I watched Lake Monona appear and disappear as the bus trundled along its route. As new riders got on, they filled the seats up front or took the forward-facing ones behind me. The space across from me stayed clear. One of the two women who'd had that intense conversation about the breakup of her marriage got on at her usual stop. I hadn't seen her with her friend since January. This morning the bus was half empty, everyone occupied, no hubbub. As slices of the lake popped up between garages and over the edge of a furniture warehouse, it winked at me cheerfully, like a confident liar.

I yanked the yellow cord, leaning over the woman next to me to get my fingers around it. We'd just passed the sign for a stop. "Let me off!" I called across the whole length of the bus, breaking the commuter's code. I could have at least said "please." I stumbled over the boots of a tall kid with his feet in the aisle and wrenched myself down the three steps to the bus's back door. I pushed the red button. The bell didn't bing, as I'd already signaled the stop. I looked up at the mirror and met the driver's frown. I held on to the railing as we bumped over railroad tracks. I pushed out of the folding doors as soon as we slowed. I didn't even say "Thank you!" to the driver, as is the custom in this nice city where I live.

I walked past a bank and a knitting store. I stomped my feet through melting puddles. I hated Ponge. He'd masqueraded as a failure, not even getting close with "Soap." He kept telling himself he'd destroy the manuscript entirely, and then he kept at it, to make a record of what he couldn't say. Yet all along he'd been able to say exactly what he meant with water.

Water is erasure, the releaser, always in motion, I thought. It's soothing. It says nothing. It can't be used as ink. It doesn't stain. Words written with water disappear when the paper dries. Water so kindly takes itself away. It doesn't mean anything. It doesn't provoke a reckoning, the way ink does. It's only water. Its marks don't last. Water is good, I thought. I had all along been hoping to end my story, the writer's story, at the water's edge. A little dash of nature for some resolution. Now here I was paying my respects to a con man.

I paused at the intersection and took a left down a side street. Around the corner from the City-County building, an officer led three men in orange jumpsuits out of the back of a van. A woman sidestepped me. I read from her expression the angry preoccupation my face must have been registering. "Excuse me," she said, hugging her purse. One more block, down the hill, a glimpse of blue drew me on. But there was no way to get to the lakeshore without going through the lobby of the Hilton.

Through the glass revolving door, over the backs of velvet armchairs, the lake flaunted itself through the hotel's giant picture windows. This way, the guests got a lake view before they'd even checked in.

The gilded doorframe mediated my long stare at Lake Monona. The water flashed playfully. It was having fun. The landscape shivered as two men and a woman pushed out the door, buttoning their nice overcoats. They were talking about coffee. Where to get it, whether they had time.

It was as if they didn't see me. They brushed past, leaving a mist of hair gel and aftershave. I started walking again, still downhill. Despite the bright sun, the shadows of the buildings cast a chill. City workers pouring out of an underground garage strode by me on both sides. They hurried, leaning forward, looking down. The air from their passage swept my cheeks. I coughed and wiped my nose on my sleeve. I shoved my hands into my pockets.

Acknowledgments

Many people have helped and supported me in bringing this book to light. I'm profoundly grateful to my early readers, Lisa Black and Morris Collins. Also for help with development of the novel I'm indebted to Sarah Blackman, Michael Mejia, and the rest of the FC2 board. John Madera has worked tirelessly on the book's behalf, and his encouragement has been vital. Thanks to Lisa Williams, Patrick O'Dowd, Ann Marlowe, and the University Press of Kentucky crew. Excerpts from this project were published in *Agni*, *Conjunctions*, and the *Kenyon Review*, and I'm grateful for the support of their editors: Sven Birkerts, Bradford Morrow, and Nicole Terez Dutton. Thanks and deep appreciation to Sara Greenslit, Krista Eastman, Barrett Swanson, Meghan O'Gieblyn, Adam Fell, Gabriel Blackwell, Jay Salinas, Donna Neuwirth, Caryl Pagel, David Isaacson, and Mickle Maher, among many others of our circle, for inspiration and creative community. Thanks as well to all the Woodwards, the Jacobsons, and to Scott.

A Note on Sources

Ink doesn't set out to give the reader any context for the statements of the detainees at Abu Ghraib that are threaded through it. I wanted to create the novel from the vantage point of the newspaper reader, the media consumer who surely could not have missed the story of the American atrocities at the prison that had been Saddam Hussein's. However, I've assumed a knowledge that belongs to people who were adult and cognizant at the right time. Pictures and witness statements about the atrocities at Abu Ghraib surfaced in 2004–2005 and then again a decade later with a fight in Congress about whether to make some of the documents public. Whether officially released or not, the story of what American soldiers and contractors did at the prison has from the beginning been remarkably visible. If the reader needs some background, I suggest starting with the Errol Morris film *Standard Operating Procedure*. Other texts that helped me put *Ink* together include Mark Danner, *Torture and Truth: America, Abu Ghraib, and the War on Terror* (New York: New York Review Books, 2004); Karen J. Greenberg and Joshua L. Dratel, eds., *The Torture Papers: The Road to Abu Ghraib* (New York: Cambridge University Press, 2005); Seymour M. Hersh, *Chain of Command: The Road from 9/11 to Abu Ghraib* (New York: Harper Perennial, 2005); and Joshua Casteel, *Letters from Abu Ghraib* (Athens, OH: Essay Press, 2008).

When I first began writing this book, I didn't know it was a book, and early versions and chapters used quotations from detainees found in the *New York Times* and on the ACLU website. Almost all the quotations from the detainee statements in *Ink* were gathered from official statements maintained on the *Washington Post* website at www.washingtonpost.com/wp-srv/world/iraq/abughraib/sworn statements042104.html.

Selected sources used in my research on ink and on Francis Ponge include Bruce Bliven Jr., *The Wonderful Writing Machine* (New York: Random House, 1954); David N. Carvalho, *Forty Centuries of Ink; or, A Chronological Narrative Concerning Ink and Its Backgrounds* (1904; New York: Burt Franklin, 1971); Richard Nelson Current, *The Typewriter and the Men Who Made It* (Urbana: University of Illinois Press, 1954); Thaddeus Davids, *The History of Ink, Including Its Etymology, Chemisty, and Bibliography* (New York: Thaddeus Davids & Co., [1860]); Mirtha Dermisache, *Selected Writings* (New York: Siglio and Ugly Duckling Press, 2017); Jacques Derrida, *Signéponge = Signsponge*, trans. Richard Rand (New York: Columbia University Press, 1984); Sarah Norris, "Typewriter Inks: An Annotated Bibliography," unpublished paper, 2006; Jean Paulhan, *The Flowers of Tarbes, or, Terror in Literature*, trans. Michael Syrotinski (Urbana: University of Illinois Press, 2006), originally *Les Fleurs de Tarbes, ou, La Terreur dans les lettres* (Paris: Gallimard, 1941); Francis Ponge, *Mute Objects of Expression*, trans. Lee Fahnestock (New York: Archipelago, 2008), originally *Rage de l'expression* (Paris: Gallimard, 1976); Francis Ponge, *The Nature of Things*, trans. Lee Fahnestock (New York: Red Dust, 2011), originally *Le parti pris des choses* (Paris: Gallimard, 1942); Francis Ponge, *Soap*, trans. Lane Dunlop (Palo Alto, CA: Stanford University Press, 1998), originally *Le Savon* (Paris: Gallimard, 1967); Nathalie Rachlin, "Francis Ponge, *Le Savon*, and the Occupation," *SubStance* 87 (1998): 85–106; Esther Rowlands, *Redefining Resistance: The Poetic Wartime Discourses of Francis Ponge, Benjamin Péret, Henri Michaux and Antonin Artaud* (Amsterdam: Rodopi, 2004); Joyce Irene Whalley, *Writing Implements and Accessories: From the Roman Stylus to the Typewriter* (Newton Abbot, Devon: David & Charles, 1975).

The song Jordan sings is "How to Save a Life," the 2005 hit by The Fray.